their stories as they grapple with the uncertainty of their imminent deaths. As readers, we get the unique pleasure of seeing the many watershed moments that change the course of a friendship from an array of perspectives. For the life of me, I can't understand how Fernanda Torres keeps this rich cast of characters and buffet of absorbing action straight. One can merely delight in the complexity of life presented in these pages, understood all the better through the lens of death."

John Gibbs, Green Apple Books on the Park
(San Francisco, CA)

"This book reveals a writer in full command of her art. In it are smells, sounds, objects, situations, reasoning, emotion, humor, complexity . . . . The author gives herself over to the mean, dirty world of her characters. Their voices are distinct . . . . The plot flows without feeling contrived, without seeking to teach lessons. The language is colorful, lively, molds itself around the characters, surges forward. This is a serious book in which humor is important: there is crudeness, the confrontation of problems, the pursuit of expression. It is through a group of old friends that Copacabana is revealed. And what one sees is the failure of a middle class who believed in the hedonism that has historically been associated with this part of Rio de Janeiro . . . . Breathtaking, a stunning debut."

Mario Sergio Conti

PRAISE FOR *THE END*

"With fast-paced language and a comedic spin, Brazilian author Fernanda Torres transforms the process of aging into a thrilling read in this story of five debaucherous male friends who, drawing near their respective ends, are looking back on their best and worst moments as we revel in their decadent amorality."

Emma Ramadan, Riffraff (Providence, RI)

"*The End* is the perfect summer release. Torres creates an aging, male Carioca friend group that is a mess of cynicism, nostalgia, frustration, and a seemingly unending appetite for sex. This book is raunchy, sophisticated, and so wonderfully Brazilian. I devoured this book in one sitting. *Parabéns* Fernanda!!!"

Daniela Roger, Books & Books (Coral Gables, FL)

"You think you see *The End* coming—or the ending coming—but Fernanda Torres has other plans for you on this journey. Torres presents five friends—fairly flawed, tragic clowns—and their views on life and those around them as they try to navigate their lives and deaths. This novel is a funny, smart, well-conceived, and perfectly executed playful look at mortality."

Nick Buzanski, Book Culture (New York, NY)

"The vibrant writing of Fernanda Torres had me completely enthralled by the lives of five self-indulgent characters, and then even more enthralled by their deaths. *The End* is an ultra-compelling dark comedy."

"Fernanda Torres animates the lives of 'five middle-class men with mediocre jobs and no artistic or economic achievements' with remarkable artistry and economy. Morbid and life filled, sobering and ecstatic, *The End* has much to show its reader about the forces that make a single life, and the community of people and places that supports that life, worth living. Come for the company (wisecracking cranks, impolitic priests, characters who have to ask, 'Who cared about boring eternity? Everyone in it would have traded a thousand years of the Lord's peace for five minutes more of earthly torture'), and stay for *The End*."

"Torres' writing [has] flair and wit . . . [an] unforgiving portrait of men at their worst."

"*The End* is an impressive and dizzying narrative that gathers meaning around the many misfortunes, climaxes, offenses, triumphs, and disappointments that constitute a life or, in this case, lives. Five friends in Rio recount

RRES

THE END

Translated by Alison Entrekin

RESTLESS BOOKS
BROOKLYN, NEW YORK

This work is published with the support of the Ministry
of Culture of Brazil / Fundação Biblioteca Nacional.

Obra publicada com o apoio da Fundação
Biblioteca Nacional / Ministério da Cultura do Brasil.

 MINISTÉRIO DA CULTURA
Fundação BIBLIOTECA NACIONAL

First Restless Books paperback edition July 2017

Paperback ISBN: 978-1-63206-121-8
Library of Congress Control Number: 2016940784

Cover design by Strick&Williams
Cover photo by Martin Munkacsi, akg-images
Set in Garibaldi by Tetragon, London

1 3 5 7 9 10 8 6 4 2

Restless Books, Inc.
232 3rd Street, Suite A111
Brooklyn, NY 11215

www.restlessbooks.com
publisher@restlessbooks.com
Printed in Canada

For my old men,

João Ubaldo Ribeiro
Domingos de Oliveira
Mario Sérgio Conti
Luiz Schwarcz

My brother and my father

CONTENTS

ÁLVARO

*September 26, 1929
†April 30, 2014

MAY THE BASTARD who invented the Portuguese pavement rot in hell. God damn Dom Manuel I and his lieutenants. Irregular stone squares beaten into place by hand. By hand! Of course they were going to work loose. Wasn't it obvious they were going to work loose? White, black, white, black, the waves of Copacabana. What good are the waves of Copacabana to me? Give me a smooth surface free of calcareous protuberances. Stupid mosaics. They're everywhere. Pour some concrete over the top and send on the steamrollers! Holes, craters, loose rocks, exploding manholes. After seventy, life is an endless obstacle course.

Falls are the biggest menace to the elderly. "Elderly," what an awful word. The only thing worse is "senior citizen." Falls are what separate old age from extreme senility. The jolt destroys the connection between head and feet. Bye-bye, body. At home, I go from grab bar to grab bar, groping furniture and walls, and I shower sitting down. Armchair to window, window to bed, bed to armchair, armchair to window.

There, another treacherous little stone out to get me. One day I'm going to take a tumble. Not today.

One day. "One day" used to be so far away. I ran into Ribeiro on Rua Francisco Sá. We hadn't seen each other in a while. He said we should get together "one of these days." The next he was dead. São Francisco Xavier Cemetery was horrific, an Auschwitz oven. The tombs looked like they were melting. I felt sick in the crematorium. People thought it was the emotion. They weren't entirely wrong. Ribeiro had been in great shape. He played volleyball until his last sunset, left the beach, and checked out in the shower: heart attack. I don't have a single friend left alive now. Ribeiro was the last. I was sure he was going to bury me. He jogged, swam, stopped smoking at forty, and refused to go limp. His sister thinks it was Viagra. Ribeiro fucked around; it was a big deal to him.

Before him it was Sílvio. Or was it Ciro? No, Ciro was the first to go, of cancer, then Neto and Neto's wife. Neto couldn't stand Célia, but he died a year after she did. Go figure. She was a pain in the ass to begin with, but when she got older, Jesus Christ . . . she was bitter, cranky, and ugly. Neto couldn't take the peace and quiet.

And to think that Célia had been such a foxy bride. She should have died back then, in her prime. If Neto had only known, he wouldn't have cried so much at the altar. Men are fools.

Sílvio departed one February, during Carnival. He started partying on the Friday and went for ten days straight. The following Sunday, he left three whores in his apartment and went out to buy more blow, mixed it with everything imaginable, and his heart gave out. They found him face-down in Lapa, near Avenida Mem de Sá, with a bottle of poppers in his hand and five Gs of coke in his pocket. Sílvio used to drink, which is no big deal, but when menopause came . . . I know, it's "andropause," but I don't like "andropause." It's like "jill off"—it's repulsive. "Jack off" is better, regardless of gender . . . Anyway, when menopause came Sílvio lost it. He met a pair of sex kittens from down south, dealers, and became their slave. We stopped seeing each other because of the *gaúchas*. They took him out of circulation. God sent two heartless bitches to finish him off. It was punishment. What year was that? I don't even know, so many have gone: years and friends.

Not all that long ago, it used to take me ten minutes to get from my place to Dr. Mattos's practice on foot. Mattos is my GP. Now it takes me forty. Walking isn't an unconscious act any more. I watch my step, my knees, and focus on the route. Everything hurts, for a whole list of reasons, all of which have to do with old age. Mattos has sent me to more than ten specialists. One wants to operate on my cataracts, another, my gallbladder, and they all stuff me full of pills. Dr. Rudolf doesn't think my veins can take the pressure and is planning to put stents in my femoral artery and my aorta. I stay quiet and pretend they're not talking to me. They're a neurotic bunch, doctors. They're vain, and brutal. I'd like to see one of them go under the knife.

Whoa! Dog poop. The icing on the cake. There's a woman in my building who breeds hysterical minihounds with high-pitched barks. She goes away every weekend and leaves them locked in the laundry room. They get lonely and yelp. I'm going to report the witch from 704 for cruelty to animals. It must be humiliating to pick up dog poop with little baggies, and I understand the people who can't be bothered, but I just don't agree with keeping dogs cooped up in apartments.

I regret every pet I've ever had. Unhappy, needy, dirty. Four dogs and a cat. The first one died of old age: blind, lame, and smelly. The cat was ripped to shreds by its father—it had a huge Oedipus complex and was obsessed with its mother. The other dogs expired for different reasons, all horrific: distemper, a tumor, poisoning. My mother had scattered rat pellets around the garden and forgot to lock Bóris up. I never trusted her again. Poor thing, she made sure he had clean newspaper, fresh water, took him to the vet, and cried as if she'd lost a child. Even so, I never forgave her.

No one is more selfish than a child. I can't stand my grandkids. They live far away—better for them. They're noisy and self-interested. I loved my daughter until she was five. After that I couldn't bear her hysteria, my wife's hysteria with her, hers with the maids. I used to do anything to avoid going home. I think the only reason I had an affair with Marília was so I'd have somewhere to go after work. I loved Marília's house. I'd kill time there until about ten, drinking and listening inattentively to her jabbering.

I didn't care if we had sex or not, but I made the effort for her sake. What I really liked was her small, but very pleasant, house in Jardim Botânico, with an outside area where she kept a few tortoises.

I've never been big on sex. I enjoyed it while it was happening, but couldn't be bothered to make the first move. And women invariably transfer to men the obligation to be in the mood. Since I never was, my lovers only stuck around as long as it took me to seduce them.

Marriage is the marital status most suited to men who, like me, don't enjoy the company of others. There's nothing more exhausting than managing dates and expectations. A bad marriage can be great for both parties, and mine was. Irene turned her back on temptation, and so did I. We lived comfortably in two bedrooms, all very sad and civilized. One day, she realized she was getting old and that it was her last chance to fuck, have orgasms, and be passionately in love, those things women believe in. I figure it was Rita's adolescence that pushed Irene over the edge. She started group analysis and did it with Jairo, the club manager. It was awkward. No man deals well with his wife's cheating. I had to stop swimming at the club. I really liked that pool, but the membership was in her name.

Irene regretted it, but it was too late. I found myself alone and guilt-free, because she was the one who'd left me. I even took an interest in two other women, unlike Irene, who was unlucky and never had another partner after the rower at the club. He was married and stopped answering her calls after a month. Women are all naive. We haven't seen each other in thirty years; we were together for fifteen. I started having problems getting it up with Aurora, my second girlfriend after Irene. I lie, things weren't going so well back when I was with Irene, but with Aurora it was definitive. I suffered for a good few years then let it go. Bye-bye, hormones, bye-bye, ladies, bye-bye, heavy silence in the room, bye-bye, eyes full of pity. I would be Franciscan. A satyr and a friar.

My dad was just like Ribeiro; he couldn't accept the fact that he couldn't get it up. I remember seeing him and my mother looking radiant one Easter, and I asked what the secret was. Dad clapped his hand down on Mom's thigh and claimed that his elixir was "this woman here." I was proud of them. On Mom's seventy-fifth birthday, she took me aside and said she was sick of trying to get Dad's dick up. It was too much work. She felt it was her duty, but she was tired and didn't want to anymore. She had even urged him to take a lover and said she didn't mind, but it made him angry. That conversation made me really uncomfortable. Irene was at the peak of her crisis, and I've always been against parents talking about sex with their kids. Mom wanted me to convince Dad to leave her in peace.

I opened the door of the room, which was all shut up, and found him in bed in a foul mood. I asked how things were going and he said, "Bad, real bad." He told me Mom was having an affair with their insurance broker. My father's dementia had made him paranoid, jealous, and delirious. He'd gone off the deep end. He accused his wife of having cheated on him with a long list of men they'd known for the entire time they'd been married. She, of all people—a virgin when they married who had never dared lust after anyone. He owned a pistol and said something about shooting her and then killing himself. I threw the pistol into the sea.

I brought her to live with me, which only deepened Irene's dissatisfaction. I became a lightning rod for family problems. Rita was held back in school that year, the cook quit, the last dog bit the dust, we had a leak in the bathroom—it was all stacked against me. We put Dad in a home in Maricá, where he died, convinced he'd spent fifty-nine years with a compulsive adulteress. Irene should have married him. They'd be going at it to this day.

And here comes a bike! Cyclists are all assassins—suicides and assassins.

When I look at myself in the mirror I see Aunt Suzel. "It's the estrogen," Mattos once told me. It makes old men look like old women and old women look like old men. Aunt Suzel died a spinster and a virgin, at the age of eighty-six. She'd spent the last twenty-six years pushing around the stuffy air of Andaraí with a hand-held fan, repeating that she wanted to die. It made you want to give her a helping hand. One afternoon, she fell down the stairs—the fall—and they couldn't put Aunt Suzel together again. She lived with her niece in a three-story building with no elevator. Now she visits me in the mirror.

Red light. There are no cars coming, but I don't want to risk stumbling. I wait for the green light like a law-abiding German. It's stinking hot. Rio has always been hot; it's nothing new, nothing to do with all this Greenpeace nonsense. I fried many an egg on the cobblestones of Penha when I was a kid. The world's been ending for as long as I've been in it.

I've only a vague memory of what testosterone is like. I don't know what it is to be young anymore; it's like talking about someone else. I never was very active. Ribeiro and I used to go out a lot, and boy, did we drink—too much. I traded day for night, put on weight, developed a solid belly supported by two broomstick legs and topped with a short neck that holds up my shiny bald head.

Not Ribeiro. He'd go straight from the nightclub to the beach. He'd only sleep after jogging from Lifeguard Post One to Six, there and back, nonstop. He kept his hair for a long time, which gave him a few extra years as the Don Juan of the beach promenade. Ribeiro never married; he taught PE and had a thing for seventeen-year-old female students. He once got a working over from one of their dads. Nowadays, he'd be behind bars. I always thought Ribeiro was immortal. But no one is.

Who will come to my funeral?

I got married after Ciro and was one of the last to get divorced. In the space of ten years, we all did the same thing. But not Neto. Neto endured Célia to the end. Poor thing, he never knew what it is to use the bathroom with the door open, fall asleep with the TV on, smoke in the bedroom, eat in bed, and not have to talk to anyone or watch the nightly soap.

I think Neto stayed married because he was half-black. I hesitate to say anything about the color of people's skin. Even Monteiro Lobato, the legendary Monteiro Lobato, was labeled a racist. But Neto, because he was half-black—go ahead and burn me at the stake together with Lobato—always went out of his way to come across as respectable. He thought marriage gave him status. I don't blame him, I get it. Is it racism? Whatever, to hell with Zumbi dos Palmares, Martin Luther King, et cetera. Sílvio, who was fair-skinned and blond with a receding hairline, didn't give a damn what others thought of him. There must be something to that.

I got used to single life quickly and moved to an apartment at the back of a run-down, old building on Rua Hilário de Gouveia. Irene got the house and I got the car. I screwed Aurora and the other one in the metallic blue Chevette. Over in Barra da Tijuca, when it was still all sand. On the way back, we'd stop at a motel and watch a porn flick. When I was able to, I'd repeat the deed. I was still into sex in those days, even though I had a hard time getting it up.

It was women who made me lose interest. Nagging, sniveling, needy. Women love to blame their own unhappiness on the next person. I never let them drag me in. The minute they get one sign of life from you, they shoot off a three-page monologue in your ear. Boy, can they talk; they never get sick of yakety-yakking. Then they turn on the waterworks so we suckers will feel sorry for them. I don't like women. Truth be told, I don't like anyone.

I did like Neto, Ciro, Sílvio, and Ribeiro, though. Men don't talk. We each say something idiotic, we laugh, we drink, and there you have it: a great night. Women are always trying to make an event out of things.

Green. This light takes forever to change and then it only stays green for two seconds. Off I go, as sprightly as Marília's tortoises. I don't believe it. It's blinking already? It's red! What did I tell you? There's still a third of the crossing in front of me and the wretched thing turns red! Who did they base their calculations on—Speedy Gonzales? What's your problem, mister? Gonna run me down? Go on, smartass, split my knee in half with your headlights. I know you want to pass, sonny boy! One day you're going to be old (with any luck, you're going to be old) and a young guy in a hurry is going to shatter your leg and you'll spend the rest of your days in an adult diaper, terrified of crossing the street. Manholes, high curbs, the stench, Argentineans.

I don't read the newspaper, I don't read magazines. I don't read. I can't see properly either. All I do is watch TV. Football, all day long. I like the after-game commentary.

I stopped at the VCR. No, that's a lie, I have a DVD player that came with the forty-inch TV, but I never did get the hang of the remote. Before that, I used to rent the odd film on the way back from Mattos's practice, but the rental shop closed. I don't miss it.

I've been fortunate enough to grow old smoking.

I don't separate my trash, I don't recycle, I throw cigarette butts in the toilet, I use aerosols, I take long hot showers, and I brush my teeth with the water running. Screw mankind. I won't be around to see what happens.

I haven't voted in thirteen years, I'm not responsible for the tragedy around me.

Detour due to road works. They love their road works. The dirty cones in the middle of the lane, cars speeding past, narrowly missing me. Don't they see me here? Jackhammer. Jackhammer. Jackhammer. How does that poor guy stand it? He's going to die young. He won't be missing anything. Well, he'll probably miss something. I don't know what, but he probably will. I've never seen death as a possibility. Not that I'm really attached to anything special in life—it's just that death doesn't exist. Death is a chronic illness.

I remember seeing Sílvio's hands shake and thinking it was a hangover. We were still young. But his son Inácio told Ribeiro at his funeral that it was Parkinson's. He said his dad had continued screwing around, and had suffered in the hands of the gaúchas, but he'd started mixing up names, the number of his apartment, the time he was supposed to take his medicine. Sílvio was slim, elegant, and bad. Real bad. Nasty. He committed suicide that Carnival. There's many a way to do it.

Women didn't give Sílvio a second glance. But all they had to do was exchange two words with him and they'd be head over heels. And he played them—he'd call lots, then stop, pretend to be seeing someone else, treat them badly on their birthdays. Women love to be treated badly.

That was in the beginning. At thirty-two, Sílvio married Norma and slowed down. But then came the kids; Norma had post-natal depression after the second and became a pain in the neck. To make things worse, Sílvio's mother-in-law moved in with them. The house became a Wailing Wall. There was bellyaching, the nightly soaps, and kids underfoot all day long, with kiddy baths, baby food, toys, runny noses, school, poop. He lost his patience, packed the oldest off to boarding school in Petrópolis, which the boy only left at Christmas, enlisted his mother-in-law to look after the youngest, said goodbye to Norma, and went to live in the bachelor's pad he kept in Glória. Sílvio wasn't rich, but he wasn't poor either. He hadn't even unpacked and he'd already arranged to meet up with three hookers, all on the day of the move. Sílvio enjoyed an orgy.

He fell hard for the gaúchas and went to live down south. We toasted his departure. We drank a lot at a party in Leme and popped some pills that he gave us. He wanted to teach us how to live. At daybreak, we were kicked out: me, Ribeiro, Neto, Ciro, and Sílvio. Five zombies and a troupe of easy women. Sílvio proposed we take the party to his bat cave. We applauded the suggestion. He started taking off his clothes the minute he walked in, saying he was hot. Ciro locked himself in the bedroom with the Argentinean—he always was a

class act. I think Neto left, and I don't know where Ribeiro got
to. That left me and Sílvio, in his underpants, in the lounge
room; plus the chick I'd brought with me, who'd been with
Neto; and Sílvio's brunette, who before I knew it was going
at it with him on the armchair with tapered legs. The other
two launched themselves at me without asking if I wanted
to, Ciro started moaning on the other side of the wall, and
the Argentinean yelled, "Faster, faster!" I was a spectacular
flop. One of the chicks, a blond from the countryside, tried
to help me along, but I gave her some money and sent her
on her way. Sílvio fell off the armchair with the brunette
and didn't get up again. Ciro must have fallen asleep too,
because I didn't hear anything from him in the bedroom. I
left at eleven with a throbbing migraine. I had a black coffee
at the bakery and collapsed on the rug in the hallway. I was
out of it for twenty-one hours.

Maybe Ciro and Sílvio did that all the time, but not me.
That was the first and last time I came close to taking part in
an orgy with friends. There's something a little queer in every
male friendship. Fucking the same women is a roundabout
way of fucking each other. And in the same physical space,
it's a fine line. But there's no way—not as a joke, not when I'm
off my face, not anytime—that I'd kiss Neto, Sílvio, Ribeiro
or Ciro. Well, maybe Ciro. Definitely Ciro. After forty, your
turn-ons shift.

Ciro used to rake them in. Women would all but sit on
his face. Ciro met Ruth at Juliano's party and decided he was

going to marry her in a church, do the whole big white wedding thing. He was mad about Ruth. She was really beautiful, and intelligent, and sexy. Ciro thought the love of his life would open the doors of monogamy for him.

It took about ten years of marriage to deflate Ciro's hard-on. And Ciro without a hard-on wasn't Ciro. He agonized and talked about it all the time. He didn't want to cheat on Ruth because he knew it was a slippery slope, but Ruth had become a mother, a wife, a companion, a sister, everything but a lover.

He started picking fights with her, ugly fights, for no reason. I don't know if he planned it or if it was desperation, but overnight he started getting irritated at little things she said, a glass here, a deodorant there. He'd pack his bags and leave over something insignificant, slamming the door behind him. Ruth would go crazy, miss work, lose weight, and so would he. After a week, he'd come home and they'd fuck as if they'd just met. It worked for a few years, and he even got his color back, until their arguments became more destructive than the previous same-old same-old. First he took a shine to Marta, or was it Cinira? I can't remember. He fucked one of the two, or both at the same time, anyway, all I know is that once the floodgates were open, Ciro laid half of Rio de Janeiro in little under a year. Ruth wasted away. Women nourish the fantasy that true love is capable of transforming men. When it doesn't happen, and it never does, they lose their self-respect and become sorry-looking shadows of their former selves.

Ciro actually managed to be worse than Sílvio, because Sílvio had never loved anyone, but Ciro loved Ruth a lot. She was so shocked by her husband's erratic behavior, his disrespect for her, and lack of patience with the family that she developed a strange kind of apathy. It all started the day she caught Ciro at Sílvio's apartment with Milena, the wife of a client of his. After that, the residents' committee forbade Sílvio to lend the apartment to his friends. That afternoon, Ruth burst through the door, shouting, Milena hid under the sheets, and Ciro scrambled for his trousers. Ciro kept his head, got dressed, and left without explaining a thing. Ruth continued yelling in the corridor as the elevator went down. Ciro took the first cab he saw and hurried home. It was amazing how cold that man could be. When he got there, he showered, put on his pajamas, and sat down to watch TV. It took Ruth about twenty minutes to arrive, possessed, frozen on the doorstep, ready to brawl. But Ciro, the genius—a bastard, but a genius—was all lovey-dovey. Ruth started on about the apartment, the whore, and, with a straight face, Ciro said he didn't know what she was talking about and swore that he'd come home, wondered where she was, and sat down to watch TV. Little by little, he began to feign restrained indignation at her having set the dogs on a couple she didn't even know and, what's more, in Sílvio's apartment! And he pretended to be worried about his wife's mental health. Less than a week later, Ruth was admitted to a clinic. Ciro never forgave himself, but he didn't do anything to change the situation either. He moved into a tiny apartment in Santa Clara, where there was no room for anything but himself. And he continued ticking off names in his little black book. He was averaging three a week, sometimes four, depending on how needy he was feeling.

I'd never thought Ciro could be so brutal. I expected anything from Sílvio, but the cold-blooded way that Ciro acted with Ruth was shocking. I had envied Ciro my whole life. He was very good-looking and one of those guys who could play pool, soccer, badminton, poker, and win at them all without any effort. And even in the most vulgar of situations, like that almost-orgy at Sílvio's place, Ciro knew how to be courteous. He took the Argentinean off to the bedroom like a gentleman.

I got married because of him. Since I was single, I started being left out of Sunday lunches. Neto and Sílvio would go with their wives and Ribeiro and I weren't invited. Irene was Ruth's friend and they introduced us. I thought it couldn't get any better than that. Afterwards, they spent years dragging us through the mud.

I thought he was losing weight because of the all-nighters and excesses. One sunny Tuesday, Ciro invited me out for a coffee and told me he had cancer of the pancreas and that there was nothing to be done. He'd just turned fifty. I was tongue-tied. I didn't know what to say. I thought about the day he'd met Ruth at Juliano's party and what a fine-looking couple they had made. Ciro was our Kennedy. He departed six months after that coffee. I avoided him. I was terrified. I didn't want to see him like that. But I carried the coffin. Ruth didn't attend.

Here come some little thugs. I've lost track of the number of times I've been mugged. At one point, I would only go out with the clothes on my body. Then, one stupid afternoon, on my way home from an MRI over in Botafogo, I was approached by two boys. When they realized I had no money on me, no cell phone, fuck all, they beat me up. Now I always carry some money for the thieves. They're gone. Maybe they were honest kids after all. Black, in shorts, flip-flops, shirtless, but honest. Blame it on Monteiro Lobato.

My dad gave me the entire collection of Lobato's *Yellow Woodpecker Farm* one Christmas. I was twelve. The books survived and I gave them to my daughter, thinking I was introducing her to heaven, but she went into a sulk because she wanted a Barbie. I tried to teach Rita math with Viscount Corncob, history with Grandma Benta, and grammar with the rag doll Emília, but she complained that there were no pictures and developed an aversion to the collection. She grew up ignorant and futile. I prayed for her not to put on weight as a teenager, because with her IQ, the best she could do was marry well.

She married so-so: a radiologist from Uberaba. His dad owned an x-ray clinic and the son followed him into the business. They met while she was on vacation in Ouro Preto. My son-in-law is a monumental fuckwit, the sort who blames everything on stress. Right, stress. A hypnotic drowsiness washes over me every time I talk to him. I could be standing, sitting, in the car, or at an insufferable end-of-year party. Felipe and Marcelo whinny loudly to wake me up and chant like retards that Grandpa's not all there. Little do they know that I'm only protecting myself from their bore of a father. The same individual who gave them half their mediocre genes, seeing as how the other half came from their mother, who inherited my worst genes, the ones that don't like Monteiro Lobato. The branches of this tree are rotten, dear Felipe and Marcelo. Your children are going to be fat like you, they'll get beaten up at school, and they'll be spoiled brats. Go on, laugh. You have no idea what awaits you—acne, small dicks, baldness, high blood pressure, cholesterol, a chronic cough, halitosis, hair in your ears, shortness of breath, urinary incontinence, a stroke—and I'll have a front row seat. Any street urchin has better genes than you two. Now go to your room, because your father's whining is making me doze off.

Rita visits me in Rio twice a year. She wants me to move to Uberaba. As if. As if I could stand Uberaba, and she me, and I her children. Give me the home in Maricá any day. I try to be nice when she comes, her idiot husband always in tow. I arrange for them to come at night, when insomnia sets in, to see if all the griping will lull me off to sleep. It's a powerful sedative, my son-in-law's blather.

My block! Another fifty-seven steps and I'm there. I love counting steps. I don't get out much. I have nowhere to go, haven't worked in eighteen years. The other day I realized I'm an employee of my health—it's a full-time job. Every month I have my monthly exams, every year the annual ones, every six months the six-monthly ones. When one's done, it's time for another. And you have to make an appointment, take the doctor's request with you, get it stamped, and get in line. Private plans are no different than the public system. Mattos's practice is in an office building here in Copacabana that's full of senile doctors. Every now and then one kicks the bucket. I go there every week, I know the distance, the time, the total number of footsteps to get there, the block-by-block breakdown, the rhythm of the traffic lights, the flower beds, the lampposts, and the stones along the way.

Now that Ribeiro is dead, there isn't anyone for me to meet up with, even if only by chance, at the intersection. The only people I visit are my doctors and I don't like them. I don't spend a thing. I rent out a shop in Copacabana that I inherited from my dad, and that pays for my health insurance. The rest comes from my pension. I eat sausages, bacon, chicken wings, and ribs, I drink water straight from the faucet, and I don't need anyone.

What's that siren? It's the fire truck. I thought it was an ambulance. The good thing about sirens is that they stop me from hearing the buzz, the swarm of bees that appeared about five years ago in my left ear and then moved to my right, in stereo, and is only getting worse. I'm going deaf. Tomorrow I have another hearing test. I think I left my glasses at home.

What siren is that now? Ah! It's a garage door. The garage of my building. I made it. I didn't even count properly, I was so busy talking. To whom? Talking to whom? To myself, since I'm the one I like to talk to. There's a car coming up the exit ramp, it's coming fast, I'd better get a move on. It's the heartless witch from 704. She's fleeing the dogs, going away for the weekend, the coward. I don't think she's seen me. No, she hasn't seen me. The car becomes airborne for a moment at the top of the ramp. She's driving like a maniac, talking on her cell. She doesn't realize I'm here. Drop the goddamn phone and pay attention to what's in front of you! Me! I'm in front of you! Ah! Finally, she's seen me, she's going to brake, she missed the pedal. How did she miss it? She's nervous. So she should be. How old is that crone? Did she pass a driving test? Can you even drive at that age? What about the dogs in her laundry room? She's braking! She found the brake, I can hear the tires squealing. The car's still moving. How is it still moving? Did it skid? Isn't it going to stop? Is it out of control? She looks at me with pity and closes her eyes so she won't see what she's about to do to me. Open your eyes, you wretched woman, come see what you've done. Why didn't I report you to Animal Welfare? I should've known that someone who treats her own dogs like that has no respect for human life. I can already feel the metal brushing my pant leg.

A leap. How many years has it been since I last leapt? I bend my right leg, stretch out my left and throw my weight forward. Go! Metal on pant leg! Walking isn't an unconscious act any more. I send the commands. Bend, stretch, I'm in the air, I prepare to land, my toes touch the pavement, I release my weight . . . the paving stone is loose? How can it be loose? I throw myself on it and it comes loose? Who was the dunce who beat it into place? Where's the contractor? Where's the mayor, who doesn't come? It's too late, my foot twists, I'm falling, the car scrapes past, but gravity is already pulling me towards the pavement. The fall. My fall, the one that will make me miss the days when I counted my steps to Mattos's practice. From one moment to the next, I'll be Aunt Suzel. My hand scrapes the ground, tries to break the fall—it can't. The skin of my elbow tears, my hip pops out, and my head plummets towards the course granite of the curb, striking it like a church bell pealing.

Black, black, black, black, black, where's white? Where are the waves of Copacabana? The hag from 704 is a dyed blond, the sort who reeks of cologne and talc and wears matching skirt suits.

My angel of death. Whoever would have thought?

I once asked a Buddhist who believed in reincarnation what actually reincarnates. He said it was something so very minute that there was no trace of the former individual in it. There's blood coming out of my head. The battle-ax from 704 gets out of the car in a tizzy, the doorman comes running. I don't feel a thing: no pain, no regret. I'm fine here. It was nice to remember my pals—nothing is a coincidence.

If there were another life, it'd be nice to catch up with them, visit Ciro and Sílvio in hell, I'd like that. But there isn't. Death doesn't exist. Not even the reincarnationist Buddhist thinks he's going to come back the same as he used to be. I'll be on a plant, in the spittle of a lizard devouring a plant, in a fly licking the spittle of a lizard devouring a plant. I'll be out there. It's been long enough, and I'm tired. This indifference suits me.

I've said bad things about women. They deserve it. Men are all worthless too. And they weren't made for one another.

I disintegrate in the air over Copacabana. I once read that death was the most significant moment in life, and it is. Mine has been good, so far, not for much longer.

IRENE WAS IMPASSIVE when she heard that the man with whom she had spent fifteen years of her youth had died. Her daughter called from Uberaba in a panic. Rita was at the airport while her father was lying in a refrigerator at the morgue. She had left the kids with her husband and wouldn't be able to make the connecting flight in São Paulo, stop by the police station, and talk to the funeral director in time to bury him that afternoon. Rita complained about her lack of siblings and asked her mother to go to the morgue to ID the body.

"I know you hate him but I don't have anyone else."

"I don't hate your father," said Irene. She was about to say she didn't feel anything for him, but thought it sounded worse than what she was being accused of. Hatred. Irene hated it when her daughter blackmailed her like she was now, forcing her to go downtown in that heat to see, of all things, one last time, the mistake. That was how she referred to him: "the mistake." Irene really didn't want to play the good mother right now. She didn't want to go. She had buried him years earlier, when they divorced, but she decided it was best to go through the motions of loss. At ten thirty she stepped out of a taxi on Avenida Mem de Sá, in front of the morgue.

The smell of rot emanated from the building. The putrid air was even worse inside. The smell stung her nostrils, working its way into her nasal passages, even when she tried not to breathe through her nose. Couldn't he have chosen a cooler day? Irene went to reception, took a number, and sat on a plastic chair to wait. The cracked seat nipped her thigh, obliging her to watch where she put her leg. The minutes that followed were interminable. Sorrow hung on the faces of those who, like her, were waiting their turn. She thought about getting a drink of water, but when she saw a cockroach dart across an electrical socket and hide in the drinking fountain, decided to go thirsty. She read the notices on the bulletin board, the messages of faith, and took down the phone numbers of two funeral directors, as Rita might need them. Lost in limbo, she was startled by a shriek coming from the corridor. An obese woman appeared, carried by two staff dressed in white. Washed over by waves of horror, she howled like a beast. The entourage crossed the waiting room and delivered the poor woman in all her delirium to a group of family members, who took her outside. The staff returned to their slow work and Irene shared their apathy. She was relieved that she was there for someone who meant so little to her. The howls from outside made her compare herself to the fat woman. The fact that she was suffering less than anyone else there was reassuring. She felt that she had one up on everyone else, a petty sentiment that was only excusable because of the strangeness of the situation. One hundred and seventeen, someone called. It was her number.

She went to the counter and from there a young man in a grubby white coat led her to the elevator. They rode up in silence, avoiding eye contact, and got out on the third floor. A long gallery of closed doors extended as far as the eye could see. Irene followed her guide to the second-to-last door on the right and waited while he fumbled with a key ring until he found the right one. They walked in. The air conditioning was better in there, but the stench was worse. The cold light flickered on the wall of squares, and, only then, watching the medical examiner go through the routine of comparing the tag number with the one on the protocol, did Irene realize what was about to happen. In one of those drawers was the phantom, her phantom.

The examiner was the one who was indifferent, not her. In this government building, Irene discovered, in dismay, moments before setting eyes on the frozen body of her ex, that she had been lying every time she played down his importance in her life. Álvaro still made her stomach churn. Her nausea had nothing to do with the funk of the place; it was the specter of unresolved regrets. She felt like throwing up.

Standing in front of the second square in the corner across from the door, the examiner motioned for her to come closer. His gloved hands pulled out the narrow metal drawer. On it lay the mistake. She hadn't seen him in years.

The light slowly revealed his nose, which looked even more hooked, and his sagging cheeks. His double chin and bald head created a halo of stiff skin around his face. His features were a flint-gray color. The drawer came all the way out, allowing her to see his wizened shoulders, his thin arms, the eternal pot belly, and his white body hair. She didn't want to look at the rest. His nakedness made her uncomfortable. She stood there in thought, studying the contrast of his buttocks against the aluminum drawer. How small he was. There was blood on him, but it wasn't that, his age, or even signs of the accident that intrigued Irene. Álvaro didn't look like himself at all. His arched mouth had joined at the corners with the creases that ran down on either side of his nose, giving him a villainous look he'd never had in life. The comical passivity of times past had given way to a scowl. He had always been miserable, but not bitter. Had he become a bad man? The dead never look like the living, she thought. Álvaro was born old, but not evil, she concluded.

When had she seen him for the last time? At their daughter's wedding? Célia's funeral? Neto's? She couldn't remember. Her conscious efforts to remove him from memory had worked. The question ushered in a second: When was the last time she had been with him? In bed with him. Snatches of their fifteen long years together came racing back, involuntarily. The separate bedrooms, his unease, his conspicuous bald patch, his anger, his paunch, his tiredness, his inertia and impotence. The only image she had intentionally preserved was of the two of them naked, wrapped in the sheets of a mountain guesthouse, where they had gone to spend the weekend in the early days of what would later become a tragedy. No affection had survived their marriage.

"Álvaro doesn't like women," she said, lying on the cushions on the dark wooden floor of a mansion on Rua Visconde de Caravelas. "He should have become a priest." Why did she stay locked away in a loveless marriage, treated like a second-class citizen by her adolescent daughter, while all her friends were getting divorced and moving on? Why was she still with him? The girl? The asthmatic dog? The maid's end-of-year bonus? She wanted to live, fuck, love, and she didn't even know if she had enough time left to learn to do it all. Couples who had much more going for them were coming to an end. Ciro and Ruth. "Álvaro's a zero, a nobody, a nothing—why should I suffer over a nothing?"

Vera was harsh. She waited for Irene to finish her laundry list of complaints, then, as the session drew to a close, said they had come to an impasse. She didn't believe they could make progress on their own. It wasn't just Irene. The same was true in all her work as a therapist. Vera was convinced that group analysis was the only way to free Irene from the straightjacket of rationality that imprisoned her. She was completely within her rights not to accept it; however, if she preferred to continue with conventional treatment, she would have to find another professional to help her. Irene listened, offended. The affected way Vera had said "straight-jacket of rationality" should have made her leave, but, at the age of forty, she was too young, too stupid, too lost, and too desperate to say no. She said yes to group therapy.

Her thoughts had wandered without her noticing. Why remember that afternoon? She had agreed to serve as a guinea pig in an experimental school of psychoanalysis, so popular back then but whose techniques, now obsolete, were like antiquated plastic surgery procedures, a breeding ground for neurotic aberrations among the generations that had served as its fodder. Irene didn't like to reopen old wounds. Even dead, she thought, Álvaro brought back bad memories.

She was objective.

She signed the form stating that the body of the scowl-ing individual before her was that of Álvaro Pereira Gomes Soares, resident of Copacabana, eighty-five years of age, white, old, and miserable. Signed by his ex-wife—mother of his only daughter, Rita da Costa Soares—Irene Azevedo da Costa. A long time ago, to her delight, separation and then divorce had expunged the Soares from her name.

When she set foot outside, the asphalt was scorching hot. One o'clock in the afternoon. The whole ordeal had lasted three and a half hours. She wanted to go home, bathe, and throw her clothes and shoes in the incinerator. She consid-ered her moral duty to her offspring fulfilled. There was no

way in hell she was going to the funeral. She had the right
to return to the paradise of her solitude.

Despite her vow, Irene attended Álvaro's farewell. Rita
insisted, sobbing through the telephone line. She complained
again about her lack of siblings. Siblings, thought Irene, one
doesn't make the same mistake twice.

She had just scrubbed off the crud from the morgue
with a long shower. The idea of getting dressed and facing
the sauna outside all over again, the decrepitude of the
cemetery, the cockroaches . . . I'm an old woman—has the
girl no compassion? Grow up! Bury your father without the
self-pity. He was over eighty! I don't pity anyone, much less
her. She's still young, she can do whatever she wants with
her life. I'm not going to throw away another dress, another
pair of shoes. I'm not going to track cemetery dust into the
apartment. I'm seventy-three, missy! I'm the one who should
be blackmailing you!

But she didn't say anything. She arranged to meet Rita at
two thirty at São João Batista Cemetery. The procession would
leave at four. She begrudgingly chose an old skirt, a black
blouse that didn't suit her, and a pair of too-tight sandals.
At least she had cleaned out her wardrobe, she thought. On
the sidewalk, she hailed the first taxi she saw. It was an old
Chevrolet Corsa with loose gears, no air conditioning, and an
exasperating funk of air freshener and construction worker's
armpit. She wanted to make up an excuse to get out, but she

felt sorry for the driver. She told him to drive on. Even as she breathed through her mouth, the bitter perfume found its way to her olfactory glands through her taste buds. She wasn't having a good day.

Chapel Ten. She climbed the stairs and went inside. There was no one there. She thought she was mistaken and did an about-face, then decided to take a look at the deceased. She got close enough to the bier to see Álvaro's scowl. It was him, the bald head, the double chin, the curved mouth, all his. She avoided looking at him again. She took a seat at one of the chairs arranged in rows, their backs to the wall. Irene counted the seconds separating her from the shower she was going to take when she got home.

No one had sent flowers, she noticed. Just a crown of white lilies with the words: "In loving memory, Rita, Cézar, Marcelo and Felipe." Who had fixed Álvaro up? She should have brought a magazine. No, it wouldn't look good. Where's Rita? Why don't you say something, Álvaro? Irene laughed at the thought. Then she fell silent.

Out of the quiet came the memory of the day she had helped her husband wrap up his old Monteiro Lobato collection to give Rita for her seventh birthday. His boyish expression, anticipating his daughter's delight, reliving his own childhood through her. Irene's eyes welled up. He was a good father, she thought, and was moved. She felt respect for and even missed the man lying motionless in front of her. She was struck by her widowhood. She was a widow. A widow, she repeated. Something she had desired so often back when they were married, that he would disappear once and for all, was now a fact and absolutely no good to her. On the contrary, she missed something and didn't know what.

A humble, respectful older man opened the door. He greeted her from a distance and went to pay his respects to the deceased. He stood leaning against the wooden coffin for several minutes, praying. When he was done, he made the sign of the cross and turned to the room. The lack of a quorum made him uncomfortable. He needed to share the moment with someone, but the only mourner present didn't look like she was in the mood to chat. Ignoring her reserve, he took the chair beside Irene's. She shuddered and pretended not to notice.

"What a shame . . . " muttered the man.

"Yeah, what a shame," replied Irene.

"Here one minute, gone the next, but God knows what he's doing."

No. It wasn't possible that, to make matters worse, she'd have to listen to a bunch of platitudes from someone she'd never seen before. Better to interrupt him.

"Were you a friend of Álvaro's?"

"I was the one who came to his aid. I've been the building doorman for more than fifteen years. Time flies. You get used to seeing someone every day, then suddenly . . . That's why I live every second as if it were the last, you never know what tomorrow will bring, life is a match that you light and you never know when it's going to go out."

Irene thought about calling for help. Clichés made her skin crawl.

"The only way is forward. There's no turning back the clock. It's God's will."

The doorman was a Gatling gun of readymade phrases. Suddenly he stopped. He must be worn out, thought Irene, and was thankful. He lifted his head and looked at the coffin.

"I lost my wife a month ago. She . . . She . . . "

His voice caught in his throat. He tried again, but couldn't go on. Irene watched the pantomime of pain, the tears that came and went, the spasms and gasps, the erratic gestures.

"It isn't right, it isn't right," he repeated, shaking, and collapsed into convulsive sobs. "I prayed to God . . . "

Irene placed a hand on the widower's shoulder so as not to do nothing. She glanced anxiously at the door. Where's Rita? Rita! I found someone to mourn your father with you!

"What about you?" asked the man.

"I'm the mother of his daughter."

"Ah . . . "

He recomposed himself in the face of her objectivity.

"We hadn't seen each other for many years. It's more for her that I'm here."

The doorman realized that his commotion had been a waste of energy and apologized for bothering her. Irene told him not to worry and the conversation came to an abrupt end. They sat there quietly, staring into space. The no-nonsense manner of Álvaro's ex-wife helped jolt him to his senses. He didn't cry again, even when the coffin was lowered into the grave.

Rita arrived almost an hour after the doorman. Her mourning had morphed into a nightmare of stamps, signatures, and copies of documents. A problem with the paperwork meant the funeral had to be put off until the end of the day. It was to be the last one.

"They almost had to make it tomorrow," explained Rita, mopping up her sweat.

Irene reined in her desperation at having to stay there another hour. If Álvaro had had friends or relatives, she could have snuck away. If her daughter's useless husband had left the boys with his mother and come to help, she wouldn't be stuck in that purgatory.

"Isn't anyone else coming?" she asked.

"I don't think so, I don't know," said Rita. "His friends are all dead, he only went out to go to the doctor, but doctors don't attend funerals, it's against their principles."

Rita thanked the doorman for coming and he acted out the accident in detail, from start to finish, indignant that it had taken so long for help to come. Without a pause, he described the neighbor's distress.

"She has heart problems, she's in a state of shock," he said. "Her son's taken her to stay with him and put the apartment on the market. The dogs are still there. It's just tragic."

"I know," said Rita.

Irene listened, bored. She felt sleepy. When the sun hides behind that building, she promised herself, I'm leaving.

There were still a good few inches of blue left in the sky, so Irene turned back to listen to the endless conversation between Rita and the windbag. The light coming through the window had caused her pupils to dilate and it took a few moments for her eyes to grow accustomed to the dimly lit interior. The ceiling went black. She felt dizzy and leaned back in the chair. She rested her head against the wall, stayed calm, and waited for her vision to return. Rita and the doorman had left the room. As a natural reflex, she checked to see if the bier was still there. It was. But the corpse was sitting up, with its hands on either side of the coffin, which made it look like a fishing boat. Álvaro was grinning at her.

"I'm so glad you came, Irene," he said sweetly. Her glottis tightened with panic; she wanted to scream but couldn't. Her hands stiffened and she struggled to open her mouth. She called for help. Then she awoke with a start.

"Mom! Are you okay?"

It took Irene a while to focus. When she came to her senses, she remembered to look at the body. The tip of his nose, the only piece of flesh visible from where she was, assured her that Álvaro was still lying down.

"What time is it?"

"Four thirty. I'm tired, I need to go."

"It won't be long now," insisted Rita.

Irene went out to the corridor to get a drink of water, took a sip, then remembered the cockroach in the drinking fountain at the morgue and decided she wasn't thirsty. She didn't want to go to the bathroom either and avoided touching anything. Even the air disgusted her. She returned to the wake.

She was standing in front of the door when someone kicked it open. It was the chaplain, dressed in character, holding a bible and looking tense. He paused and shouted, "Who's next?"

Rita, Irene and the doorman turned around in surprise. Not satisfied, the chaplain repeated the question, "Who's next?"

They stood staring, open-mouthed, as the cleric uttered his ominous words.

"Who called this clown? Rita, was it you?"

Irene looked the chaplain in the face, exasperated. If nature was fair, she'd be next.

PADRE GRAÇA rose before dawn. He prayed, bathed, ate only a little, as always, and prepared a small valise with liturgical objects. São João Batista Cemetery awaited him. For twenty-four years he had fulfilled the task of taking God's word to families who had lost their loved ones. In the beginning, he had seen meaning in being a chaplain, but not anymore. He wished he could be transferred to a small community where people were still religious. Urbanites were hostile; they no longer believed in eternal peace. His enthusiasm as a seminarian had given way to a sterile isolation, with no way out. He dreamed of celebrating weddings, baptisms, anything but that. Too much contact with death had made him insensitive. He was no longer suited to the job. He had requested a transfer months earlier, but his superiors didn't appear to be in any hurry to find a replacement. Padre Graça waited in resignation. For this reason, he was overwhelmed at the prospect of a sequence of funerals on what promised to be a long, hot day. Had he lost his faith?

No one seeing him enter the building in Botafogo would have suspected the battle being waged in the silence of his soul. The idea of abandoning the cassock seduced him, especially at night, like an insistent demon. He had always dismissed the thought, but, more recently, he'd spend hours tossing and turning, unable to push away the treacherous desire. He would be a teacher, a nurse, a bank clerk, and would answer to God himself, without having to impose Him on anyone. He was tired of the crusade against the friendly fire of the evangelicals and the enemy fire of atheists. The battle was lost.

It was riddled with doubt that Padre Graça began that morning's service, praying for the soul of a great-grandmother of seven, grandmother of fifteen, mother of four, and widow of one. Although sad, the relatives seemed resigned to the departing of their matriarch. They were practicing Catholics and made an effort at mass. He briefly forgot his current discontent with his job. Afterward, he thanked those present and confessed, "I came here without hope, I leave with it redoubled."

The following services reduced that morning's communion to ash. A teenager, a young mother, and a loving father. Of the five deceased, only the old woman that morning and an old man at sunset followed the natural logic, the order that should prevent mothers from burying their children, babies from being deprived of their mothers' love, and fathers from being absent in hours of need. Once again dismayed at the number of times God appeared to have been asleep on the job, Padre Graça succumbed to pessimism. I'm God's undertaker, he muttered to himself.

As the day was dying, he bitterly climbed the stairs of the chapel on his way to room 10. At one point he slowed his pace, certain that he was incapable of offering any comfort. I'm the one who needs consoling. Who will do it for me? That was when the opportunity, the idea, the temptation arose. It was a priest's duty to remain firm precisely when the flock was at its most vulnerable. Vulnerability in the face of death was auspicious for revelation. His mistake lay in his passive benevolence. What good was mercy? Catholicism should elect firmness as its ally. I am a priest, he thought, but I castrate myself by donning the skin of a sheep. May I show no kindness. I will be ruthless, virile, Roman, warlike, and rapacious. The terrible side of the divine being. May the Old Testament be my guide.

And, certain of his new conviction, he stalked into room 10 at a quarter to five that Tuesday afternoon, stopped on the doorstep, and bellowed his cruel question, "Who's next?"

Padre Graça fell silent and stood there, holding the door, not sure if it was the beginning or grand finale of the service. Proximity to the end should have inspired a heightened awareness in the living, but there was no sign of such elevation here. The stupefied looks of those within earshot expressed only their disapproval. Padre Graça's eyes came to rest on an elegant elderly woman who was looking at him in dismay. It was Irene. The next to go. Padre Graça regretted his outburst, gave a little nod, and left without closing the door. He walked down the stairs to the front office. There was no one left to pray for. The day was over. So was his career.

IT WAS THE LAST STRAW. Irene had no reason to stay there listening to the affronts of a prayer boy to the dead, wasting precious minutes of her life to bury a man who had been born old. I have to go, Rita! Where's Cézar? Why didn't he come to help you? What marriage is this, where you can't make the sacrifice?

But before she could say it the gravediggers came for the coffin. Irene accompanied them. She walked through the lanes to one end of the cemetery, where they buried Álvaro in a simple grave.

As she passed through the gates of Tartarus on her way out, she hurried to a taxi. Collapsing into the back seat, she turned her head to one side and watched the traffic through the window, the hustle and bustle of the living. She examined her own hands, the hands of an old woman, her visible veins and wrinkled skin. She was over seventy, but she didn't see herself like that. She missed her father doting on her, her mother's face, the house in Cosme Velho. How good it had been to feel safe, and how hard to lose her certainties. Adolescence had taken away her grace, school her innocence, and men her sweetness. No one recognized the princess in her anymore, just her, there, in a traffic jam on Rua São Clemente.

The burial, the wake, it hit her all at once.

How much time did she have left? She didn't need much. She was tired, had no plans, and wouldn't mind departing. Not even her daughter needed her anymore; in fact, they rarely saw each other. The last thirty years had been devoted to absolute solitude, a lack of romantic prospects, not depending on anyone. She had managed. She didn't long for a partner anymore, anxious to complete every stage in life: dating, studies, work, family, children. She had done it all as best she could.

That night she had a dream.

She was on the beach. The sun was setting behind Morro dos Dois Irmãos, the weather was pleasant, the sea calm. Álvaro was kneeling before her in swimming trunks, his back in silhouette against the orange sky. He was slim, strong, and good-looking. He smiled at Irene.

"I'm glad you came. I'm glad, Irene."

And he kissed her. Then they stayed there like that, arms around each other. A little further along, in front of the country club wall, a circle of people were watching them. It was her analysis group. They were talking about her but she couldn't hear what they were saying. Álvaro asked if everything was okay and turned his wife's head so she'd be looking at him when she answered. Álvaro had become Álvaro. He was flaccid, bald, shriveled, and couldn't get it up.

Irene opened her eyes and couldn't sleep anymore. The next day she took her daughter to the airport.

RITA SEEMED PROUD to have completed the Herculean task. She talked about her father as children do after funerals, with great ceremony. In her words, Álvaro acquired a greatness he had never had in life. Napoleon, crowned with defeats. Irene listened—it was her job to listen. Children rarely take much of an interest in their parents' suffering; they guard the role of victim jealously, unwilling to relinquish it for anyone. It was time for Rita to tally up her achievements and for Irene to appreciate her daughter's maturity. She pretended to. When they parted, she hugged her daughter, remembered her as a baby—the future she'd imagined for her, the tears, the fears, the fights—then she looked at the woman in front of her. Rita had grown up, accepted a modest existence in an inland city, with a man who was mediocre, but solid, faithful, and present. She hadn't taken any risks, nor had she wasted any time. She had enough of her father's bovine passivity to be content with the boys' soccer victories, the nine o'clock soap, and Carnival at the club. She was happy, much more than Irene. And from Irene she had inherited her pride. She bowed to domestic life, but not to her husband. She had been successful where Irene had failed; she knew how to control her impulses and to be satisfied with her dissatisfactions. Rita fulfilled the two great obligations of the modern world masterfully: to be young and active. She worked out at the gym every day, ate properly, and moisturized at night. She did the bookkeeping for her father-in-law's clinic. She was solid, upright, pragmatic like her mother, simple like her father, and good at accounting. She had eliminated doubt. She had no aspirations beyond buying a new car, organizing Felipe's and Marcelo's birthday parties, and putting on Sunday barbecues. Irene looked down upon and admired her daughter's achievements. At any rate, she had turned out a lot better than her atrocious adolescence had indicated.

Rita's skin had broken out in pimples, her hips had grown broader, and her belly, which was cute at four, was worrying at twelve. At the end of her fourth year, Irene had been called in to the school. They wanted Rita to repeat the year. The same thing had happened the following years. Decembers were spent trying to make up grades, shouting and sitting by her side for hours on end, drilling equations and irregular verbs. Rita liked to laze about watching TV and eating crackers with cream cheese. She wanted to be like the soap opera heroines and be kissed by the leading men. The worst was yet to come, when she abandoned the soaps and stopped bathing. She only bought secondhand clothes, walked around in flip-flops, and didn't shave under her arms. She listened to Led Zeppelin at a volume the whole neighborhood could hear and answered all questions angrily. She abused her mother, making fun of her clothes and opinions. Irene was her archenemy. After flunking the first year of high school twice, she finished her studies at a school for adults, Fast, where there wasn't even a roll call. She paid and passed. She didn't try to get into university. All seemed lost. After graduating from Fast, to celebrate no one knew exactly what, her parents paid for her to take a vacation in Minas Gerais. Fifteen days in Ouro Preto in the company of some equally bizarre girlfriends. Irene thought she was crazy when she left the three of them at the bus station.

Rita lost her virginity in Ouro Preto, at the age of eighteen, and came back a different person. She began to date Cézar and everything about her mellowed. Unlike her mother, Rita was terrestrial, satiable in love. She got married at twenty-one, after a long engagement, and went to live in Uberaba. She had two sons and now she had just lost her father. Her mother was still alive and well, thank God. Rita wasn't given to speculation. She'll die in peace, thought Irene, which is really something. And she hugged her daughter, this time with the respect she deserved.

Rita disappeared through the gate and Irene found herself lost at the airport. She hadn't traveled in a long time. Would she ever do it again? Irene was left alone with her frustrations. She decided to enjoy their company in public. She sat at a counter and ordered a coffee, to wait until the plane had taken off.

—

"And why do you think you hit your daughter?"

"I don't know. She came home drunk saying she needed money and got dressed to go out. It had just turned dark. I told her I wasn't going to give it to her, but she opened my bag and took a wad of notes without asking. She did it in front of me and marched off down the corridor. I thought it was too much, so I stood in front of the door and ordered her to put the money back. She gave me a shove and tried to turn the key in the lock. I tugged on her hair and her head hit a corner of the door jamb. I don't know what I did. I knocked the key out of her hand and slapped her, I think it was on the face . . . but . . . I don't remember . . . I don't remember. She's always been ornery."

"What about you, Irene? Are you ornery?"

Irene stared at the Holy Inquisition. The faces of those present showed explicit pleasure that she had accepted the role of defendant so readily. The group's mirth grew with each of her failures. Irene had admitted that she was flawed and weak, making everyone else feel better about themselves. Vera's question was a clear insinuation that the source of Rita's hysteria was her. They were all waiting for the atonement, the mea culpa that, as the theory went, would free her of the psychological wounds that kept the door to happiness closed. The bubble. Irene would have to admit, before the jury, that Rita's aggressiveness had its origins in her neurotic mother, her sexual frigidity and unacknowledged envy of everyone else.

"The problem is that marriage of hers."

"She needs to get laid."

"Who? Mother or daughter?" laughed Roberta. Roberta, of all people, with a husband who beat her and a son who was a drug addict. What are you laughing at? thought Irene.

"Do you think maybe Álvaro was a flop with you because you were a flop with him first?"

"You're all a flop. That's why the girl is the way she is."

"You need to get laid, Irene. And by somebody who knows what he's doing."

The last remark was delivered by the group's alpha male, an attractive, seductive alcoholic. There were suspicions that he was having an affair with Vera. The analyst had undergone a big transformation; she had lost weight and started wearing skirts, high heels, and lipstick. The change had coincided with the arrival of Paulo, who never talked about himself and amused himself with everyone else's psychodramas. Paulo liked to end attacks on Irene with ironic, always sexist remarks, wisecracks about the neediness of women and the glories of the penis.

"You're a classic case of a woman who isn't getting enough," he would say, suggesting that he would know how to resolve the problem, although he had no intention of doing so.

Irene came out of the sessions in shreds. Vera had barely intervened. It was as if her therapist had left her naked in the savanna to be devoured by carnivorous lizards.

When she left the elevator, she hid her face, which was swollen from crying. She decided to walk. Botafogo was so ugly. It didn't used to be, but it was now. She didn't want to go home. Álvaro's mother was there because of her senile husband who'd accused her of adultery and was planning to put a bullet through her head. She was a good mother-in-law, quiet and discreet, but she'd been sleeping in the study for a month. She spent the day in the kitchen and the living room, cooking and watching TV. She liked cooking, which had been Irene's salvation when the cook quit, the only tiny bit of respite among so many disasters. Rita was well on her way to flunking for the third time and even the dog was on its last legs at a veterinary clinic in Copacabana. He was old. He'd been Rita's eighth birthday present, after the Monteiro Lobato fiasco. The animal could no longer see. He stank, limped, and had intestinal issues. He lived in a corner of the laundry room and it would have been a blessing if someone had called to say he'd gone to a better place. The night she'd had to jump out of bed to rush him to the pet hospital, unconscious, she had considered asking for him to be put down, but her Catholic upbringing had gotten the better of her. How good it would have been to hear that Major wouldn't be coming back. But he did. So he could die by our side, said the mother-in-law, all choked up. The elderly are moved by anything. Irene wished she could throw him out the window, but she just smiled and pretended to be happy about the dog's extra time.

Now she was wandering aimlessly through Botafogo, with nowhere to go. If she could, she'd have shed her skin, left herself behind, changed her name, started all over again. Until the age of thirty, Irene had thought it was all a rehearsal. She observed what happened around her and went along with things, but when her daughter was no longer a baby, she realized that the future was defined early on. Rita was insecure, fussy, and fat, and not particularly bright. It had never occurred to Irene that her maternal dreams might not come true, not for her or for her off-spring. She could admit that she had chosen the wrong man, profession, friends, but she had carried with her the arrogant conviction that she would make an example out of Rita. She had failed.

The girl was enrolled in a traditional school—Catholic and strict. She would be a lawyer or an economist, her mother predicted. When she was learning to read and write, however, her poor handwriting, difficulty reading, and inability to understand the basics of mathematics were a sign that things weren't going the way they were supposed to. Her small learning problems soon took on catastrophic proportions, and to avoid having her repeat the year, her parents decided to change schools. They chose Jean Piaget. Irene sent her to an experimental institution in Jardim Botânico and went to parent meetings—talks on freedom and creativity, and the importance of discovery and the pleasure of learning as opposed to dictatorial teaching methods, which are top-down and shove subjects down the students' throats. On the first day of class, she left Rita at the new school convinced that the problem wasn't her daughter, but the system. Her certainty lasted less than a semester. In June, Rita received a terrible assessment from her teachers and school psychologists. If the school had report cards, she'd have gotten Ds. And to make matters worse she'd become agitated, rebellious, refused to eat sitting down, jumped about, and drew breasts and penises compulsively. The interminable homework of her former school vanished at Jean Piaget. Concerned, Irene made an appointment with the school psychologist. The psychologist explained that children should only do their homework if they were motivated to. Essays weren't compulsory either. Irene laid out her arguments for discipline and her worries about Rita's passivity, but none of it was of relevance to the psychologist. Something else was worrying her.

"Here it is," she said, pulling a piece of paper out of a pile of drawings. It was a doodle by Rita, a penis strung up by the glans with "Daddy" written beneath it. Beside it was a spiny creature, somewhat like a pink porcupine, flashing two angry eyes and a mouthful of sharp teeth. Underneath it said "Momy."

"Maybe some family therapy is in order," she said, and ended the meeting.

Wandering down Rua São Clemente, Irene tried to accept that she had lost control. She tried to separate her own pride from whatever became of her daughter, but it was hard. She compared Rita's development to that of friends' children—her peers, all sane, strong, and healthy—and the inferiority of her offspring was a cause of suffering. I bred wrong, she thought. A knot in her throat forced her to stop. She sat on a low wall, dizzy and gasping in agony, feeling like she was suffocating. Where could she escape to? She remembered the club; she still had it in her to relieve her nerves with a swim.

She swam two thousand meters without thinking a thing. She climbed out of the pool feeling better and showered in the changing rooms. Because she had left her membership card at home, she should have stopped by reception beforehand to get a stamped authorization to give to the lifeguard. But she had pleaded that they allow her to take care of the paperwork after letting off steam and they had agreed. Now she climbed the stairs to management, glad to have something to do, something else to put off going home. An athletic man of about fifty, tanned and helpful, took care of things for her. His name was Jairo. He criticized the club's strict rules. A beautiful woman like Irene didn't deserve to be treated like that. Irene blushed. She'd heard so few compliments that she barely remembered they existed, so that "beautiful" made her knees weak and jump-started her heart. She smiled, bright red, and lowered her eyes. She was fifteen years old again. She started going to the club on a daily basis, always forgetting her card. She would climb the stairs as soon as she passed through the turnstile, get her authorization from Jairo, and head for the pool, where she swam with cadenced strokes while fantasizing about rendezvous with her new object of desire. The title of manager gave Jairo the air of a king, and he began to accompany her to the swimming pool. Later, they arranged a set time to meet at the entrance, so she wouldn't have to go upstairs. He would go with her to the turnstile and tell the staff to let her though. On the third week, Jairo asked Irene to start bringing her membership card, as he was being pressured from higher up. Nor did he see any reason for using silly pretexts to hide his desire to be with her. Irene almost passed out. She didn't know what it was to be courted anymore and had turned her back on romanticism. Jairo had everything that Álvaro denied her. He was manly and straightforward. The afternoon she started bringing her card again, he insisted on walking her to her car afterward. He was leaning in the window, and Irene was about to start the engine, when, without warning, he slid his hand up the nape of her neck and took a handful of hair. He asked her to meet him at a bar on Rua Farme de Amoedo at six. Irene didn't reply. Suddenly self-conscious, she put the car in reverse and almost took the barrier gate with her.

The Agris was a run-down little building with a veranda at the end of Farme de Amoedo, almost in the favela of Cantagalo. The conversation didn't last long. Jairo knocked back his whiskey, pulled a bank note out of his wallet, and placed it on the table as a tip. They left with their arms around each other, she anxious, he focused, both full of lust. The hotel was three blocks away. They went to room 304, at the back. The sheet smelling of disinfectant, the little bar of soap in the tiny bathroom, none of it was what Irene had fantasized, but it was a first step, a stance, a beginning. He came; she didn't, despite her efforts, but she wasn't frustrated. On the contrary, she stared, enchanted, at Jairo's face as he came, above her, because of her, in her, and she left, floating. Jairo walked on the traffic side of the sidewalk to protect her from the cars and called a cab. Before opening the door, he gave her a long kiss, then asked the driver to take it easy. He knew how to be a man.

Irene received applause at the next group analysis.

The separate bedrooms alleviated any potential awkwardness. When she got back from seeing Jairo, Irene didn't have to go to bed with Álvaro. In the morning, all she had to do was listen for the sounds of the shower and doors closing in order not to cross paths with him. They rarely saw each other. Her husband, preoccupied with family problems, was relieved by her unexpectedly good humor. If it was good for her, it was good for him.

They had been sleeping in separate beds for two years. It had happened by chance, after a fight—yet another—occasioned by Sílvio's digs at Álvaro during a Sunday lunch at Ciro's apartment. Sílvio had been drinking and decided to crucify Álvaro. Dripping with venom, he said that Irene had chosen the worst of them. He listed off Álvaro's bad habits: his snoring, his lack of ambition.

"Álvaro can't even beat us in spoof," he exclaimed, and roared with laughter.

Ciro told him to shut up, which only made the snake's tongue wag harder. He listed off the women who had rejected Álvaro. There had been Bete, Cláudia, Mina, Sandra, Paula, Maureen . . . Even dingbat Dora had said no.

"I was surprised you said yes, Irene. You deserve better."

It would have all been forgotten if it hadn't reflected Irene's secret frustrations so precisely. She put on her nightgown and climbed into bed, furious. Álvaro came out of the bathroom, pulled on his pajamas, and snuggled under the blanket as if that afternoon had never happened. Irene exploded. She wanted to know why he had taken all that humiliation without a fight, did he have any idea what she was going through? How ashamed he made her feel. All the things that were missing. Álvaro apologized for existing and said he'd do whatever she wanted, the way she wanted it, whenever she wanted it. His answer made her even more irate. She took out a sheet from the cupboard, a pillow, made up the bed in the guest bedroom, and ordered him to sleep there that night. Álvaro obeyed and never returned to the master bedroom. The only reason they didn't break up was because Irene was more afraid of solitude than of dissatisfaction in love. She liked hearing the sound of the key in the lock when Álvaro came home at night, his presence as father, the household expenses split down the middle. And she had no illusions about her chances of finding something better. Unlike Ruth, Irene never knew what it meant to have men falling all over themselves for her. It had always been like that for Ruth—in elementary school, in high school, and especially in college. They had studied language and literature together. Ruth had married the best of the five, and she, the worst, even though she was an attractive woman. She never understood it.

Álvaro was Ciro's friend. Ruth sang his praise, talked him up to Irene. Irene was tired of being alone and hadn't been serious about anyone for over a year. Her last boyfriend had moved to Spain. She had considered going with him, but she'd have had to give up the classes she was beginning to teach, her life in Brazil. They had promised to give it a go long-distance. Their correspondence had lasted a few months and then suddenly dwindled. He married a woman from Andalusia the following summer and she never heard from him again. Álvaro was all wrong, but had a twisted, self-deprecating sense of humor, which charmed Irene. Why not? She had never loved him, staying with him as if she were waiting for the next streetcar to come past and rescue her from her little detour—but it never came. Time, chance, and their friends in common kept them together. Álvaro chose the ring, Ciro helped, and one sunny Sunday, with Ruth and Ciro as witnesses, Álvaro asked Irene for her hand in marriage. The wine was good, the autumn afternoon, what did the groom matter? I'll say yes, she thought, I can leave him later. Let's see what happens. The years went by and she kept waiting for someone to wrench her away from Álvaro. Jairo. Jairo would set her free.

How silly she was, she thought, as she watched her daughter's plane take off over Guanabara Bay. It would have been good to be on it.

SÍLVIO COULDN'T HIDE his glee at the news.

"A little bird told me your wife is planning to run off with a guy from the club. Wake up, my friend, 'cause these women are hot to trot," he said, finishing off in English with, "They're willing and able!"

The little bird was none other than Paulo from group therapy. One of the Casanova's favorite pastimes was giving the crowd at the beach the dirt on his fellow group members. Vera liked to discuss the sessions with him in their frequent rendezvous, often in her office. She loved his frankness, his self-confidence, his self-respect. He was an alcoholic, it was true, but besides that he was perfect. She was in love, she had lost her composure. They bitched about the group, laughed at everyone's desperation, and were as happy as could be.

All it took was one drink at the Coqueirão beach kiosk for Paulo to spill the beans from the last few therapy sessions. The scandalmonger's overtime with his therapist had enriched his vocabulary of certainties. Ever since the affair with Jairo had taken off, Irene's private life had become his favorite soap opera. Paulo could smell his equal from afar.

"Jairo? He's a total sleaze," he said, reveling in the opportunity to watch from the front row as Irene fell into the womanizer's web. "The stupid woman's going to give it up next week, I'm telling you. In one month, this Jairo guy's going to stop taking her calls; in two, she'll be begging that limp-dicked namby-pamby of a husband to have her back."

After this prophecy, he tossed back the rest of his beer and headed for the volleyball court.

Ribeiro knew Paulo by name. They had a friend in common, also a lifeguard. Ribeiro preferred the crowd that played beach volleyball in front of Rua Miguel Lemos, in Copacabana, but this day he had accepted an invitation to play doubles at the Coqueirão, in Ipanema. He and his partner shared the court with Paulo. Before the game, they had the drink that got his tongue wagging. Irene's name was the first thing that caught Ribeiro's attention. The husband who couldn't get it up, the hysterical daughter, and the dying dog erased all doubt. It was Álvaro's wife, *his* Álvaro. Ribeiro hated being party to the imbroglio. He'd have to do something, but what? He needed to share it with someone. Ciro had been Álvaro's best man. He wanted a more impartial opinion and decided to consult Sílvio.

Sílvio was in ecstasy. He wanted to infiltrate the group, start therapy, get to know that Vera woman, an analyst so open to experiences. Ribeiro was in a dilemma about whether to tell his friend or not. He remembered the time he'd bad-mouthed his cousin's ex-girlfriend, never imagining they'd get back together the following weekend. They ended up married with three kids, and Ribeiro was left out in the cold.

Sílvio played counselor, arguing that he wouldn't be able to look Álvaro in the eye without telling him the truth, and practically begged Ribeiro to let him play Cassandra and break the news. Ribeiro granted him the mission, happily freeing himself of the burden.

*   *   *

Álvaro didn't like the beach. He went because everyone else did, but he stayed on a folding chair under the beach canopy, reading the newspaper and drinking mate tea. He rarely went in the water, but when he did he brought back a bucket of water to clean the sand off his feet when he was leaving. One bright morning, there he was, reading the sports section, when Sílvio came over and took a seat in the shade. With a troubled expression, he told him about Irene's infidelity then rattled off his "willing and able" to show off his broken English. Álvaro hated Sílvio for taking pleasure in something as pathetic as washing his dirty laundry amidst the commotion of Lifeguard Post Nine. Now he understood why Irene had been so cheerful lately, the reason for her light spirits; she was leaving. But Paulo from group therapy had been spot on: in one month she would return, confused, asking him to take her back; a year later she would hit perimenopause and fall into a deep depression. She would emerge from it just fine, two years after that, but she would never be with another man. It was the beginning of the end of Irene's sex life. Things wouldn't have been terribly different if she had stayed married.

With a serious face, Álvaro packed up his tent, beach mat, and chair, put the newspaper in his bag, retrieved his flip-flops, hat, and bucket of water, and turned to face the beach promenade. Before crossing the scalding sand, he gave Sílvio a solemn look and wished he was dead. But that wouldn't happen for another twenty-five years.

SÍLVIO

*June 13, 1933
† February 20, 2009

"GIMME FOUR 8-BALLS. And the poppers, too. How much is that? Do you take checks? Nope. One hundred . . . sixty . . . two hundred and five . . . two hundred and seventeen . . . I've lost count. How much? Only three 8-balls for this much? What about the poppers? Well at least throw in the poppers, for fuck's sake . . . It's Carnival!"

I'm getting the hell out of this dive, man. I hate dens, I always think they're gonna kill me. Here. No one's coming. What the fuck have they cut this coke with? Ground glass. Fuck it. Where the hell am I? Rua Evaristo da Veiga. Evaristo da Veiga . . . Evaristo da Veiga . . . Where's Evaristo da Veiga? What kind of sadist gives his son a name like that? The world is lost. Where's the aqueduct? Where's the fucking sea?

La la la la . . . Check out the hair on Zezé . . . Could he be? . . . Could he be? . . . A fairy! I love that song. Where're the poppers? Weee-aaaw-weee-aaaw . . . What the fuck! I fell over but I'm still standing . . . I'm really off my face. I need to get a taxi and get back to Suzana . . . Is she there with . . . with . . . or not? . . . No, Suzana . . . Su . . . zzzz . . .

I'd been married to Norma for three years. She hadn't been a virgin for three years. Norma wouldn't give up her

73

asshole, only went down on me out of obligation, and had lost that fear of spreading her legs that used to drive me wild in the beginning. I was trapped, I knew it, but still hadn't decided what to do. I was in the garden at Ciro's place, thinking about the puppy-dog eyes that Norma had made at me while holding Neto's baby in her arms, when the crackpot appeared. She smiled like a little kid, lit a joint, and turned her face to the sun.

"Suzana."

"Sílvio."

"Sílvio starts with 'S' too," she said.

"That's true," I replied.

She passed me the joint and I took it.

"Are you a good friend of Ribeiro's?" she asked.

"Very," I said. And we went quiet, looking straight ahead.

"What do you do?"

"I work at Banco do Brasil."

"Wow."

"Dad wanted me to stay at Itamaraty, but I couldn't handle all the gayness."

"Gayness?"

"The diplomatic service is full of fags."

"I like fags," she said.

"Me too," I said, and we laughed together. "What about you?" I said, handing back the joint.

"What about me?"

"What do you do?"

She blew out smoke and replied, "I'm Ribeiro's girlfriend."

I've always looked down on Ribeiro. Ciro always came first, then Neto, Álvaro, and—way down at the bottom of the list—Ribeiro. Ciro was heroic, Neto was conservative, Álvaro was tragic, and Ribeiro was just plain stupid. A thick-skulled virgin layer. "What's so good about virgins?" I'd ask him. He said it was a matter of preference, but the truth is that no woman with more than one neuron would have been able to withstand Ribeiro's company. Why is this girl with him? I wondered.

Speak of the devil . . . Ribeiro came to ask her to put out the joint because Célia didn't like it. I laughed; it was too ridiculous, the way his jaw dropped when he saw the two of us together. Suzana cracked up laughing too, handed me the roach, and left on his arm. Ribeiro stared over his shoulder as he walked away, an angry ape. Oooh, I'm so scared!

Eleven thirty at night and I was already in bed when the phone rang. Norma answered and said it was the bank. I thought it was weird. It was Suzana. She said Ribeiro was making her life hell because of me and that she had nowhere to go. I invented a wire transfer from Japan, a telex that was going to arrive at the office, and arranged, right there under Norma's nose, for Suzana to meet me at the branch on Rua Primeiro de Março. Norma bought it and off I went. I sped through the tunnel toward Avenida Presidente Vargas.

Suzana was standing on the corner in front of Candelária Church in a miniskirt so short you could see the color of her panties. Green. I stopped next to her, she opened the door in a huff, flopped into the passenger seat, and gave me a French kiss that made me see stars. It took me by surprise. I looked her straight in the face, unable to think about anything else but giving it to her good, and headed for my bachelor pad in Glória. We groped each other in the car, in the elevator, and had sex at the door, eight hours after meeting in Ciro's garden.

We went at it until she fell asleep, exhausted. By then it was pretty late. I put on my suit, shook her hard, and told her she had to go back to Ribeiro because I didn't want any trouble. We started seeing each other regularly, Ribeiro got more and more jealous, Suzana became more and more Suzana, and I, more and more bored with married life.

That was when Norma got pregnant for the second time.

I blacked out. I'm face-down on the sidewalk. It stinks of piss. I think it's me. No, it's the gutter. No, it's me *and* the gutter. I'm completely numb. Get up, Sílvio, move along. I've got to get a taxi. Son-of-a-bitch anxiety. It's going to be a rough comedown. I've got some benzos at the pad. I've got to get back. Where's a taxi? *In the sky the morning star appears* . . . Morning star means the party's over. It's getting light . . . the sky . . . indigo. I hate dawn. Fucking son-of-a-bitch anxiety. Where's the ground glass? One more line, just to get home. Here come some little hoodlums, fuck it.

There are taxis in Cinelândia, there are taxis in Cinelândia, there are taxis in Cinelândia. In Cinelândia. Which way is Cinelândia? *You have no mercy on me . . . La la la . . . Your eyes make me dizzy . . .* I'm always dizzy. I'm always dizzy, I go into a trance when I'm high, I've always been like this. I started smoking when I was twelve, drinking at thirteen, and was popping pills by fifteen. I lost my virginity to a hooker, a cousin took me, my dick wasn't even fully developed. I love sex. I had the Carlos Zéfiro collection of erotic comics and went to the red light district with my cousin Valdir on a regular basis. Me and Valdir gave each other a lot of hand jobs. The poor bastard died young, of tuberculosis, he was only eighteen.

I was a good student and Dad got it in his head that I should try for Itamaraty. In the prep course, I met some rich kids who really knew how to have fun. The wealthy are way more perverted than the poor. They've got no morals. Those kids had none. I was accepted into the group because of an anesthetist, introduced to me by Valdir, who supplied the prescription drugs. They brought the whiskey and each of us had to bring two girls to the parties.

One of them, Miranda, was underage. It was Fausto who brought her, saying she was his cousin. No one questioned how old the girl was or wasn't—if she was there with Fausto, she was no angel. It was the first time I'd seen two guys give it to a girl at the same time. Fausto and Bernstein. It blew my mind. I was so turned on I still had a boner at the police station. Miranda's parents had the police follow Fausto and we all wound up in the lock-up at the police station.

I was kicked out of Itamaraty. Dad was desperate and got me a test at the Banco do Brasil with a director he knew. They found a way to cover up the incident, I passed the test, and was set for the next fifty years of my life. All I had to do was show up, and the rest—pension, Christmas bonuses, other bonuses and holidays—would come on a silver platter with years of service. Far from the diplomatic aristocracy, life was much more boring. The female tellers wanted to get married, the female managers, start families, and the men only came when their team scored a goal. Best not shit where you eat, I thought.

Some folks are getting out of a taxi over there on the corner by the municipal theater. One more line. Crappy coke. Last hit before I get home. Weee-aaaw . . . weee-aaaw . . . Fuck! Fuck! Fu . . .

Norma was pretty, petite, and naive—a farmer's daughter. They lived in Ribeirão Preto. She came to spend the holidays in Rio and my mother asked me to be her chaperone. I took her up to Sugarloaf Mountain, to the Christ statue, to the beach. I took her for ice cream, introduced her to my friends, and it was weeks before she gave me a kiss, lips only. I played the hopeless romantic, acting like I didn't expect anything of her and that I was lovesick and depressed at the idea of her leaving. I was bored with the easy lays. They were vulgar, brassy, and most had been to bed with every guy I knew. Norma's virginity became a fetish.

It was impossible, back then, to exist without fulfilling certain rituals. Marriage was the main one. I recognized Norma's potential to be a geisha. She'd be so thankful to me for rescuing her from the boondocks that she'd put up with anything in order to save her marriage. Norma was my ticket to freedom.

My mother wept at the news.

When I lifted up her wedding gown after the reception, completely off my face, Norma was shaking like a leaf. I became a beast and took the poor woman like a pagan bull. Then I collapsed beside her and snored. During the night I heard her crying. It's okay, I thought, I'll worry about it tomorrow. When I sobered up, I treated her better and life went smoothly. My outings with my friends were sacrosanct. The uncertain work hours, too. I wasn't born a saint. Dad died and left me a bit of money. I bought the pad in Glória, a suburb a few towns away—my refuge.

Norma went out a lot to take Inácio to the playground, the beach, the doctor. I'd arrive home in the morning, sleep until late and, just after dinner, I'd head out. We lived like that for two years without her noticing my absence. Women like Norma only have eyes for young children. Everything was just fine until Suzana came along.

Someone told Norma's mother that I was having an affair with a hippie from Bauru and she told her daughter. Norma was nine months pregnant. With a mother like that . . . She went into labor and almost lost the baby. Vanda was born purple; it was a nightmare. When she got back from the hospital, Norma was a mess. Her mother moved in to help out. Whenever she saw me she'd look away in indignation. I stayed in that hellhole until I couldn't take it anymore, then I sent Inácio to boarding school, hired a nursemaid to look after Vanda, bid the mother-in-law farewell, and headed for Glória.

Like the song: *In Glória* . . .

Suzana in the morning, Suzana in the afternoon, Suzana at night. With Suzana I made up for lost time. Valdir, the diplomats, the benders, it all came back full strength. And better, because I wasn't a kid anymore. The day I moved, Suzana prepared a surprise. She invited over two girlfriends from Bahia who helped me put the mess in order. Then they took off their clothes and fondled each other on the sofa while I watched.

Suzana straddled me to bid me welcome. That woman was out of Ribeiro's league. The only one up to the job was old Sílvio here.

Hot flashes, palpitations, shaking. Parkinson's. I need my medicine. That poison they call medicine. People are milling around. "Back off, for fuck's sake! No, I don't know my name.

Stop bugging me. I'm not going to tell you my name!" A son
of a bitch dressed as a zebra wants to help me up. "Leave
me alone, quadruped! I'm fine here." Where? Where am I?
Why is there a guy dressed as a zebra trying to help me up?
A Colombine . . . a tranny . . . where the fuck am I? Why is
it so cold? "Zebra! Hey, zebra! Someone! Call an ambulance
and tell them to put me out with propofol. Only propofol will
do it! The one Michael used to take! Jackson . . . Five . . . "
They're gone. Thank God, they've left me in peace.

My son dragged me off to hospital the day I showed up naked
in the foyer, asking for a light. I wanted to light a cigarette. I
didn't do anything, just gave him my hand and let him lead
me away. Parkinson's does away with your initiative. I don't
know how Inácio can still feel anything for me, I did everything to make him hate me—I never did get it. At the clinic,
they turned me inside out and gave me the verdict: from that
point on, I'd have difficulty walking, talking, eating, thinking,
sleeping, and fucking. Great. And you have to pay to hear
shit like that. I was sorry I hadn't gone to the hospital sooner.
Some exams require anesthesia, the kind that you only get
in the best specialized wards.

The treatment for Parkinson's is far worse than Parkinson's
itself. And there's no cure. The drugs give you a racing mind,
cold sweats, and brutal panic attacks. The doctor stamps
the prescription and sends you home hand in hand with the
Incredible Hulk. They're a sick bunch, doctors. Carbidopa

25 mg, levodopa 250 mg, benserazide hydrochloride 25 mg. Before the pharmacist can give you the bundle, you have to show them your social security number, driver's license, electoral enrollment card, police clearance, photograph. It's easier to buy a gun and kill yourself. And that's not counting the antidepressants, antispasmodics, antacids, and the like. I got hooked on all of them. After a month, along came the hallucinations, exhausting deliriums about cars driving backwards, cuts in time, and blackouts. A whole new world. Ah, if only Valdir were here! Poor guy, he only got to try amphetamines and alcohol, he missed the best of the party.

"Get lost, drunk! Hound's breath. Piss off, go! Take a hike! Where's the zebra?" *This year isn't going to be . . . like the last . . .* My god, the cops are breaking up the last Carnival blocs. What about you, Sílvio? You staying here? At least sit up, have some dignity. Giddiness, nosebleed, fucking shit coke. The ground's wet. That's better, head up. People don't crowd around if you're sitting. Boy, does Rio de Janeiro stink. It always has. "Piss off, mongrel, go pee on another lamppost, I was here first."

I gave up everything for Suzana—my friends, my job, I lost money, everything. She and Ribeiro were always at each other's throats. Suzana spent her days hiding out in Glória with me, making up excuses to give up the night. Whenever the gang asked if I was going to introduce the mystery woman, I'd change the subject and Ribeiro would just about lose it. Suzana wasn't the sort to sit around waiting for anyone. She'd leave without telling me, say she was going to meet me and not show up, threaten to make up with Ribeiro; she'd even say she was expecting his child just to make me suffer. Suzana was one of my own.

When Ribeiro finally kicked her out, Suzana caught a cab straight to Glória. Brites came trailing after her. She was a plump blond from down south who arrived by bus with a stash of weed that she was going to sell in Rio. I told her she could stay if she gave me half in exchange for the rent. They had no other option, so they agreed. Ciro wanted to buy a third of what I had. We shared the bed, Suzana, Brites, and me. I told Ciro, Ribeiro, Álvaro, and Neto that I was involved with two gaúchas and that I was planning to move down south. Ribeiro shot me daggers from the other side of the table. He hadn't seen Suzana in six months and it was obvious that one of the gaúchas was her.

Suzana and Brites knew lots of people. All die-hard bisexuals, with a boring spiel about the world being divided into bis and the repressed. The commies didn't spend their time on sex, unlike the bis, who fucked like crazy. Brites was in love with a fag from the Dzi Croquettes who I think was named Ciro, too. I watched that crap more than ten times. The two of them liked to play Elis Regina singing "Dois Pra Lá, Dois Pra Cá" on the turntable and dance up close, imitating

Lennie Dale. It was all a big freak show; no one distinguished between male and female. Total anarchy.

One day, Brites showed up with an invitation to a fancy party in a penthouse on Flamengo Beach. I thought she was bullshitting, but she explained that she was going to make a delivery and that the host, a millionaire painter, was going to let her in. The three of us went, along with thirty Gs of coke.

We took the elevator up and rang the doorbell. The music was at full blast, no one came. After ten minutes of waiting, nothing, so we turned the door handle and discovered it was unlocked. We crossed the massive foyer and went down the main corridor, following the music and voices. When we turned into the living room, behind a marble column, there were enormous windows overlooking Guanabara Bay. A hundred naked people were entertaining themselves majestically. We entered the court of the Sun King, the splendor of Versailles. We didn't leave until the next morning and walked through Aterro do Flamengo Park to get home. We had sex all afternoon. I was thankful for having been born when I was, in time to enjoy that sexual liberation. I was never the same again. I said to hell with Christian suffering and reinstated the glory, *In Glória* . . . of the old Roman Empire.

The Roman Empire. What's this guy in a toga doing in front of me? What's he supposed to be?

"What are you supposed to be?"

84

"Hercules," he says.

"Where's your club?"

Hercules asks if I've got a light. Hideous breath.

"Yes, Hercules, I've got a light. Have you got a cigarette?"

We exchange pleasantries.

"Just what I needed, this Marlboro. I've got some blow, want some?"

"No thanks . . . " Hercules trails off.

"What about poppers?"

He wants poppers. Hercules takes a whiff and returns the flask, then off he goes down Rua Evaristo da Veiga, imitating a siren. Evaristo. What a fucked-up name.

I don't have legs anymore, or arms, I don't even have a head, I've lost my extremities. Screw the taxi. I'm staying here. Tomorrow Suzana will come and get me. I wonder if she's already gone. It wasn't her, Sílvio, it was another girl, girls. Suzana never came back. Cry, go ahead and cry. You left three pussies in the apartment and went out to buy more blow. Suzana never showed her face again. God, I miss it all.

I had an epiphany in the penthouse in Flamengo. I owe it to her. It was Suzana who made me understand that men were born to be free, and fuck, and come, and merge with other arms, asses, tits, thighs, and cocks. I don't really remember what happened, just the ecstasy, the fulfillment. That night was a game changer, the peak of something that separated me definitively from Ciro, Neto, Álvaro, and Ribeiro. It was the end of my youth. In that neoclassical sitting room, with my tongue in Brites's cunt, as she kissed Suzana, who was getting it from a blond guy with a beard, who was fondling the tits of the Japanese girl from São Paulo, who was admiring the jumble of bodies on the sofa in front of her, I thought: This is the pinnacle, the high point of my existence. I decided, there, to abandon once and for all the manual of good behavior, which stops you from having sex with your friend, your friend's wife, your friend's mother and father. A bunch of sissies who don't know the pleasures of amorality.

I wanted to seduce Ruth, Irene, and Célia. As well as Ribeiro, Álvaro, Neto and, of course, Ciro. I actually tried with Irene. She'd been dumped by Jairo, the club manager she'd been having an affair with. I sniffed out my prey, called her up under some pretext or other, invited her out for a coffee. When I rubbed my foot against hers under the table, she gave me a slap, stood, and left, offended. Frigid idiot.

Her and all the rest of them. A tacky, uptight middle class, living under house arrest with their parakeets and their neutered dogs and cats. Tragic. The only thing worse is the crowd at the bank. They actually manage to exceed the bovine stupidity of my friends. Ricardo. Little Richie climbed the management ladder at the downtown branch. He was the incarnation of a new kind of employee, the economist just out of diapers, clean, pressed shirt buttoned up to his neck, tortoise-shell glasses, and a sense of ambition the size of Brazil's financial crisis. Ricardo took office when the currency changed to the *cruzado novo*. He arrived kicking the door down. I don't think he even had any pubes. He demanded returns. What returns?! The currency's worth zip. We're bankrupt, Ricardo! The government's lassoing cattle in the pastures to fill supermarket shelves, and along comes this little brat wanting to be productive, demanding balance sheets, projections, and targets from public servants who have taken solemn vows, before the flag, to never lift a finger. Didn't he get that that was the whole point? To get a job in public service and not have to strive for anything? Little Richie had hissy fits in the corridor and flapped his hands with dissatisfaction. I was the only thing standing him between him and Brasília, where he wanted to be a part of those shit plans for economic reform that always went to the dogs. My slowness was the direct enemy of his efficiency, my bare minimum, my not giving a shit about the brilliant future that lay before him. Go get fucked in that square little asshole of yours, Richie. I'm sure you'll enjoy it.

The suit, the business district, the watercooler talk, nights out with the four, it all seemed like a big failure. There was just Suzana, she was the only one who got me. Why bother with the rest? Why not do to them what I did to Norma? To Inácio and Vanda? Give them all the flick.

Every three months or so, it was never exact, Brites would go to Porto Alegre to buy drugs from a Bolivian. Suzana suggested we go with her the next time. We could go to Gramado, drink *chimarrão*, go riding in the pampas. I said yes on the spot. In the deflated state I was in, it was my salvation. I told Little Richie that an uncle of mine was on death's doorstep. "Soon, I'd have to make an urgent trip." He was actually overcome with emotion at prospect of being rid of me. I really was going away on a trip, but I told my friends that I was moving down south. Even I was surprised by my lie. Why had I said that? Why did I need to sever ties with my chums like that? It was loathing. I hated that they wanted to be everything I despised. Nothing new was coming out of there. It was the end. One of many. I went on the trip, came back quietly, and asked for a transfer. Little Richie could barely hide his glee. He offered me the Niterói branch. Perfect; every day I would drive over the Rio-Niterói Bridge and wouldn't run the risk of bumping into them. I didn't want to leave Rio. Niterói was as far as I intended to go.

The Bolivian took his time to make contact. The wait gave me time to think. I couldn't just up and leave. I needed to make a mark, provide proof of all they were losing by choosing normality. My chance came at the birthday party of a socialite in Leme. It was a golden opportunity for me to exit in style, leaving a lesson for those ignorant plebs, slave to their shitty little lives, barely managing to juggle marriage, work, and whiskey on the weekends. The party would be the beginning of something that would end in an orgy, in Glória, at dawn.

Brites prepared the arsenal and she and Suzana arranged to spend the night elsewhere; they knew how important that night was to me. I really wanted Suzana to be with me, but Ribeiro wouldn't have been able to handle it. I looked after them all, handing out spirits, narcotics, and speed to warm up. I managed it until we were kicked out by the bodyguards. Neto had taken off his clothes to pay homage to the birthday girl. He kept quiet about what he had between his legs, but when he got drunk he insisted on displaying the goods.

On the sidewalk, I finished off the rest of what I had in my pocket and suggested we head to Glória. *Glória* . . . I was heralded as a hero. We got into our cars with some bimbos and I don't remember how, but Ribeiro ended up in the passenger seat of mine. I only noticed he was there when I made a U-turn in front of the Hotel Glória. I'd been concentrating on the steering wheel while the brunette with fake eyelashes stuck her tongue in my ear. Ribeiro asked me point-blank if I'd fucked Suzana. He was curt, irritated. I laughed. What else could I do? I was headed for the grand finale of my farewell ceremony—we were about to have a fuck fest in Glória—and he comes out with, "Did you fuck Suzana?" Even Norma would have used the occasion better. Ribeiro opened the door of the moving car, the brunette screamed, and he threw himself out. I was going slowly. I drove off with the door open and didn't waste another two seconds on the dickhead.

At the pad, Ciro gave it to the Argentinean babe in the bedroom. I thought it was rude. It was my going away party, for fuck's sake, he could at least have invited me to watch. Neto must have backed out on the way there. He had the biggest guilt complex, by far, and was incurably, earnestly monogamous. Álvaro, obviously, couldn't get it up. Ciro was the only one who called the next day to wish me luck.

I went horseback riding, dropped acid, stuffed my face with barbecued meats, pulled all-nighters drinking chimarrão and bought three ponchos: one for me and one for each of the girls. We fucked a lot underneath them since it was cold; it was really good. It was the childhood of my old age.

Because no one ever went to Glória, I didn't have to change my routine. I drove over the bridge to Niterói from Monday to Friday and, from Friday to Sunday, hung out with the camp crowd from the theater, Brites's friends. The other four were dead to me, along with my salad days.

Where am I now? On Evaristo da Veiga. What kind of fucked-up name is that? Are my teeth chattering from the cold, or is it the Parkinson's? It's the Parkinson's. My doctors told me to cut out the excesses. My liver, pancreas, gall bladder, lungs, brain, they're all hanging in there by the skin of their teeth. Mephisto comes to collect. What a pretty little devil . . . "Stick me with your horns! Stick me with your horns!" She didn't hear me.

*　　*　　*

Brites was arrested on one of her many trips to and from Porto Alegre. She filled two suitcases with coke from the Bolivian and thought it was safer to come by bus, as she'd had two close calls at the airport and wasn't taking any more chances. Didn't do her much good. She rode for fourteen hours on a semi-sleeper only to end up detained at a police post on the Paraná–São Paulo state border. It would have been less painful by plane. She'd have served her sentence in Rio and Suzana wouldn't have gone after her. Brites was transferred to a prison in the interior of Rio Grande do Sul. Suzana was devastated. She packed her bags and left for Pelotas that very night. She loved Brites. And I was alone again.

The incident in the foyer made my son want to be the father I'd never been to him. He hired a psychiatrist, a physio-therapist, a speech therapist—it was awful. I told him I preferred the money to that endless trial, but he refused and paid the specialists himself. Big bucks down the drain. Inácio tried to control me in every way he could, until I put my foot down. I explained to my saintly son that we were cut from a different cloth, as they say in English. That the neat little life he dreamed of for himself was death to me. That I had supported him, working for that bank my whole life, and now it was his obligation to help me with my vices. I said that I was grateful for the health insurance, but I was no one without my blow, my whiskey, and my weed. That if

I had to live sober I'd rather he shot me dead right then and there and sent me off to Hell. Or are you under some illusion that Heaven awaits your beloved father, Inácio?

For Heaven's sake, I stuck the kid in a Catholic boys' school for ten years—I still don't know how he didn't turn out a faggot—and now he wants to treat me like his son? To each his own. It's his goody-goody mother's fault. It must be revenge, that has to be it. The medications, the exams, it's all revenge. It has nothing to do with compassion. Human beings aren't motivated by good intentions.

I forgot Norma even existed, her and Vanda. They're back in Ribeirão Preto. Inácio tells me a thing or two. He said his mother married a relative and Vanda an engineer; she's got a son. Engineer, what a mediocre profession. My dynasty was born and dies with me. No one's following in my footsteps.

Footsteps. People are milling around again. "Fucking hell, stand back, can't you see it's muggy in here?" I fell over, I didn't see it happen. Wasn't I sitting up? When did I fall? I'm going to do another line. Poppers and a line. A line and poppers. For the journey. What journey, Sílvio? Yours ends here. I'm afraid. I must be in a bad way to have pulled such a crowd. "Fuck off, you, gimme those poppers! Give 'em back! They're mine! I went to the den to get them. I'm gonna snort this shit right here in front of you, you dickhead, oh yes I am. Weee-aaaw . . . "

—

Again, it happened again. Sprawling and standing, at the same time. It's a poetic scene, me and the Carnival-goers: pirates, Bacchuses, and vampires. I like it. My God, what a relief, what lightness, what a glow, what a beautiful sunrise over Guanabara Bay. It's what I've always wanted, to not care about the things around me, to not suffer, not feel. God, it's good.

I believe in punishment. Which is a way of believing in God. Crooked, but it is. My lineage is ancient and perverse, of debauchees, devilry, and the likes. Paradise is of no use to me. I prefer the company of those who have practiced violence against others, themselves, God, art, and nature. My own kind. Divine death is my empire. It's what I've been looking for all my life. I got it. So why am I, now, in the delirium of my final moments, gripped by thoughts of damnation? Is it masochism? Perhaps. Who would have thought that you, Sílvio, would prove to be a dyed-in-the-wool Christian? There's no such thing as pardon.

Padre Roque felt me up from the fifth to the eighth grade. He liked to punish us with Dante. We'd read and reread his circles during recess, in the heat of the library. He can't even imagine the value of that long-ago torture at this hour. I owe to him the imagery that accompanies me now, as I hover over the Corcovado near the dome of the sky. There are no cherubs or seraphs, no bolts of lightning, doves or white clouds. I see the Wood of Suicides and the boiling river of blood, I see beasts, centaurs, and sodomites. "In the middle of the journey of our life, I came to myself, in a dark wood, where the direct way was lost . . . "

I went in as I came out. Man doesn't change, he transmutes, he is always the same. Until the next eternity.

INÁCIO ORGANIZED his father's funeral service. Neither Norma nor Vanda attended. The three women Sílvio had left at his apartment came to pay their respects, and stuck together the whole time. It wasn't the first time they'd been called out by the Sex Fiend of Glória. A transvestite and a few other dregs of society completed the small group. Ribeiro didn't know anyone. Sílvio's son stood beside his father's body the whole time and made a point of thanking every lunatic, drunk, bum, and whore for coming. Inácio was admirably composed, but when he saw Ribeiro walk over, he hugged his old acquaintance and broke down in tears. Ribeiro tried to reciprocate. He remembered Inácio as a child, on Sundays at Ciro's, and how he'd felt sorry for the kid when Sílvio sent him to the German boarding school in Petrópolis. He gave him a tight hug.

Inácio had been getting ready to take his youngest daughter to the children's street parade when he received the phone call. He'd been trying to contact his father since Monday. He'd made more than twenty phone calls, all ignored, and had even left a message with the doorman of the building in Glória, but Sílvio had disappeared. It happened sometimes, but the worsening of his Parkinson's, his goddamn addiction, and his depravity condemned his only relative who gave a shit to live in a constant state of worry.

"Here comes my pain-in-the-ass son wanting to control me. Chop me out a fat one so I can toast Saint Inácio, Maritza!" the madman would exclaim every time 9634 5888 flashed on the screen of his cell phone.

A stranger asked who was speaking and wanted to know if Inácio was alone or if there was someone else with him. Inácio was suspicious, thinking it might be a kidnapping, and threatened to call the police. Then the person on the other end introduced himself as a paramedic. He was calling from a cell phone found in the jacket pocket of an unidentified white male, about seventy years of age, bald, slim, and of average height. He appeared to be drunk, was in possession of illegal substances, and had been found by Carnival-goers in Cinelândia, near the municipal theater.

"We redialed the number of the last missed call. Do you know someone by that description?"

"Yep. My dad."

It's a waste of oxygen to go into the legal pilgrimage required to recover the body of an addict who checks out on a street corner in a big city. Something straight out of *Antigone*. Inácio had to deal with the truculence of the police, the sarcasm of the coroners, and the sadness of having no reason to be proud of his father. He struggled not to give in to lethargy. While he waited to claim whatever was left of

Sílvio from the cold chamber, in the same wing where, years later, Irene would go to ID Álvaro, Inácio ran his eyes over the pamphlets at reception to anchor himself to something concrete. One of them contained suggestions for funeral notices, medieval crosses, Stars of David, exalting words of love and unity. The wife, daughters, sons-in-law, and beloved mother of so-and-so thank everyone for their sympathies. Inácio didn't know what it was to have a family like that. There at reception, where Irene would later be relieved that she was suffering less than the obese mother, made queasy by the same nauseating smell, Inácio made a decision. He would publish a large half-page ad, if possible, as big as he could afford, notifying everyone of Sílvio's death. In it, he would apologize for his father.

He got a pen and a sheet of lined paper from reception and drafted a solemn death notice. The Heart of Mary next to the name of the deceased in bold, followed by a text copied from the templates he had seen in the pamphlets. He wasn't happy with the result. He kept the heart and the name, but realized that the farewell to his monstrous father should be on par with what he had done in life. He was frank. And vindictive.

In the obituaries section of *O Globo* on February 23, 2009, a large notice, taking up almost a quarter page, caught Ribeiro's eye. He habitually glanced through the death notices and often came across someone he knew, but Inácio's name and, above all, the content of the notice, surprised him. Beyond a doubt, the Sílvio in the notice was Sílvio—*that* Sílvio, the infamous Sílvio.

INÁCIO, son of

SÍLVIO MOTTA CARDOSO JUNIOR,

wishes to communicate the passing of his ill-famed father, unfaithful husband, abominable grandfather, and disloyal friend.

"I apologize to everyone who, like me, suffered affronts and insults, and invite you to his much-awaited interment,

which will take place on February 23, 2009,

at São Francisco Xavier Cemetery,

Rua Monsenhor Manuel Gomes, 155,

in this city of Rio de Janeiro, at 4 pm."

The resentment of times past, the spite, the betrayal: there it was, pounding in his temples all over again. The sudden feeling of revulsion made Ribeiro drop the newspaper. He walked across the sand and threw himself into the sea. It had rained a lot the day before and the water was filthy. The coldness of the water brought on a state of paralysis in Ribeiro, who floated there amid orange peels and plastic cups and bags. A Godsend, this cesspool. Once he had recovered from the news, he let his conscience act. He decided that he would accept Inácio's invitation and celebrate the end of Sílvio. He wanted to be sure he was buried six feet under in a well-sealed coffin.

Ribeiro had never forgiven Sílvio. In the moral order of his backward mind, not coveting your neighbor's wife was the first commandment to be followed by men who considered themselves brothers. But there was a second reason, furtive and unspeakable, propelling Ribeiro to the cemetery: to see if Suzana would be there. Now that Sílvio had gone, and Neto and Ciro before him, the only one left was Álvaro, who had already told him he didn't know a thing. Suzana was the only answer to the question that had gnawed away at him for thirty-three years. Had they cheated on him, or not?

SUZANA HAD FLED BAURU. Her family wanted her locked up for dating another girl from high school. They kissed at school, at the movies, at the ice cream parlor, and had spent the night in the police lockup more than once. Her father would roar in his country accent, "That isn't norrrmal!"

And she would reply with the same rolled "R", "It is norrrmal, Dad! It's norrrmal!"

One night, after a beating with his belt, Suzana jumped out the window, walked to the highway, and hitched a ride to Rio on a truck. She was seventeen.

The beach was a meeting place for gays. Shy ones, slim ones, chic ones, rude ones, fat ones. Suzana had friends in various circles up and down Copacabana Beach. Her wonderland extended as far as the Coqueirão beach kiosk, in Ipanema. "It was God who brought me here," the open-minded country girl would repeat, laughing, with the April sun setting behind the pier, lighting up her white teeth. Suzana loved the gay crowd of Ipanema, she shared their outlook on life. She'd grown up a hippie and an outcast, among people who looked down their noses at her. That was why she was accepted immediately and became confidante, disciple, sister, and daughter to many. She was one of them. She worked as a waitress, a receptionist, a shop assistant, and a checkout girl, and she tried her hand at acting and singing. Suzana was eclectic, but she never really got anywhere in anything.

The drag queen Lana Ley rented a back-facing one-bedroom apartment over the Alaska Shopping Arcade. She missed the sister she had left behind in Maceió and made Suzana her darling in Rio. She liked to stroll down Rua Joaquim Nabuco with her, giving her tips on etiquette. Copacabana, according to Lana, was the beach for poor gays. Something very different was happening at Farme de Amoedo, in Ipanema, in the hedonistic worshiping of Barbies and pretty boys, in the high spirits, topless sunbathing, and free sex.

Ribeiro arranged to play a game of beach volleyball near the Coqueirão with Ciro and Neto. The king of Miguel Lemos was coming to grips with the new era, although he lamented that everything was unisex now. "I'm from the days when men liked women," he would say, depressed by the scrawny macrobiotic-fed bodies. A more violent spike sent the ball into the middle of a long-haired group. Ribeiro came over to say sorry. He wasn't good-looking, but his body was impressive. The gays all applauded. Suzana got up to return the ball. She was holding a joint and offered it to Ribeiro, but he turned it down. "I don't like pot or coke, just spirits," he said. She laughed and asked if she could be of assistance in anything else. Naughty, naughty. They hit it off in bed and the bodybuilder took a shine to the beach babe from Bauru.

Both Ciro and Sílvio got married, Neto and Célia were expecting, and Álvaro, the only one besides Ribeiro who was still in the game, was sweet on Ruth's friend Irene, who, years later, would cheat on him for all of Rio to know. That was when Lana Ley kicked Suzana out of her cubicle. The girl wouldn't pick anything up, ate whatever she saw in front of her, didn't lift a finger to do the dishes or pay for anything, and was always in the company of a girl called Brites. "The freeloader!" Lana complained at the Sandalus Nightclub. Suzana moved into Ribeiro's apartment without him even noticing it. By the time he did, she was already there.

Neto's son Murilo was born in March. Ciro had everyone over for lunch to celebrate the new arrival. Ribeiro thought it would be good to take Suzana, show them that he was with someone. So he did. Suzana lit a joint in the garden. Célia was shocked—Neto's wife was square. Ciro gave Ribeiro an ironic look and Ruth signaled to him to tell his girlfriend it wasn't going over well. Irene disappeared into the kitchen with Norma, Sílvio's wife. Álvaro still hadn't arrived.

Ribeiro went to ask Suzana what was going on. He was surprised to find Sílvio sharing the joint with her in the middle of the ferns. Sílvio had never been trustworthy. Ribeiro told her to lose the roach. She and Sílvio laughed together as if Ribeiro were a hall monitor. He grabbed Suzana by the arm and left, offended. From that afternoon on, the certainty that Sílvio was having an affair with Suzana began to plague Ribeiro like a sharp, recurring migraine. Suzana hated to be put against the wall. Yeah, right! she'd reply in a fury. I did Sílvio, Ciro, Neto, and even Álvaro. Happy now? But the goddamn woman refused to put his mind at rest.

It took a long time for Ribeiro to work up the courage to ask Sílvio. He took his last opportunity before the immoral bastard left town, that notorious night after the party in Leme.

THEY WERE GROWN, desperate men, living out Rio's macho heyday and sensing its inevitable decline. They were about to see off Sílvio, the libertine, the only one of the five who was divorced. Sílvio had split up with Norma two years prior and was free to pack his bags and go wherever he wanted. The night out was a farewell. The next day, Sílvio was moving to Porto Alegre in the company of two gaúchas who, according to him, had made him young again. "Keep your marriages, he ribbed them, your perfect little lives, 'cause old Sílvio here ain't ever coming back!" The she-devils had stolen him from his four friends. Ribeiro suspected that one of them was Suzana. He was almost certain. *Almost*, but not enough, which is why he hesitated to confront his rival, afraid of looking ridiculous.

Sílvio had planned his epic send-off with strategic precision. They would lift off from his place in Glória, mixing whiskey, blow, weed, and amphetamines, and would keep their adrenaline in check, alternating between uppers and Mandrax or Lorax, depending on preference. They would cut loose at the fiftieth birthday party of Gorete Campos do Amaral, the former Madame Juneau, in her exuberant ten-thousand-square-foot penthouse in Leme, fruit of her recent divorce from the owner of a chain of French supermarkets, the magnate Gilles Juneau.

The open bar was scheduled for nine. They arranged to meet at ten in Glória and head to the party between eleven and midnight. Gorete's birthday promised to be a good one. The socialite, whose millionaire husband had traded her in for a Russian girl thirty years her junior, had decided to put to rest the role of exemplary wife with a big bash. She had dedicated twenty-five years of her life to others, but now her children were grown and Gilles was gone. She had wallowed in barbiturates for a year and needed to prove to herself that she was back in the saddle. With a bank account proportionate to the size of her husband's guilt, she splashed out on her reentry into Rio's high society. Her guests, a mixture of old money, jetsetters, starlets, sports stars, intellectuals, and counter-culture idols, didn't include the five middle-class men with mediocre jobs and no artistic or economic achievements. Brites had gotten them in at Suzana's request. The DJ, charged with providing the party favors, had ordered thirty grams of cocaine from Brites and had done her the favor of putting all their names on the list.

The Horsemen of the Apocalypse had rolled up to the party as high as kites. Ciro was the first to break away from the mother cell, attending the come-hither stare of an Argentinean woman who was devouring him with her eyes in the library. Sílvio let it all hang out on the dance floor with John Travolta moves. Álvaro leaned against the bar, while Ribeiro ordered a vodka and went to check out the view from the balcony; it was hard for him. Neto was nowhere to be seen. Sílvio kept an eye on his friends. If he saw signs of flagging energy, he'd race over with the right pill and, voila, the puppet would come back to life. If they appeared to be racing, he'd calm the monster with quaaludes. And so the hours passed, between increasingly confusing highs and lows. Wild Saturdays. Sílvio looked after the others until he could no longer look after himself. Those with masochistic tendencies sank into the Italian sofa, the maniacs reached the stratosphere. Neto was on the moon. They had been in different corners of the party for some time when he opened the bathroom door with his fly undone and, singing the chorus of the Bee Gees' "Stayin' Alive," shimmied into the middle of the dance floor with his dick swinging as a tribute to the hostess. Álvaro finally got off his ass. Ciro abandoned the Argentinean, Ribeiro, the balcony, and both ran to control the old goat. Sílvio saw that it was time to wind up phase one of their spree, but before he could do anything, four security guards trained in Israel immobilized Neto with an arm lock and dragged him to the back door, together with Ciro and Ribeiro. They were kicked into the elevator, received by a second battalion of Mossad agents in the garage, and ejected into the bed of yuccas in front of the elegant building. Álvaro, Sílvio, and a selection of first-class meat came down the guest elevator. Sílvio handed out the last round of narcotics and suggested they all head to his pad in Glória. They accepted the invitation with cheer—everyone but Ribeiro, who was doing the math. There was one broad missing for each of them to be able to look himself in the mirror when he got home. The possibility of having to share one with Sílvio—him of all people—made him want to puke. Even so, he hurried to get into his rival's car, God knows why . . . The brunette climbed into the back seat and the others got into their cars with their respective companions. Today, I'm going to settle this, Ribeiro swore to himself, and rode in silence as Sílvio drove through Aterro do Flamengo Park.

The girl was licking Sílvio's ear, while he tried to keep the car moving in a straight line. Near the airport, Ribeiro blurted out, "Sílvio, did you fuck Suzana?"

Sadist that he was, Sílvio sneered.

"Is the gaúcha Suzana? I know it is! Tell me to my face!"

Sílvio's face twisted into a grimace, his mouth opened and his teeth protruded forward as he guffawed. Ribeiro wanted to grab the steering wheel, crash the car into the first lamp-post, die, and kill the monster at the wheel and the ho in the back seat. He decided to hurt himself instead. He opened the door of the moving car, jumped out, grazed his knee on the asphalt, and went home to torture himself. He and Suzana hadn't been together for six months.

His jealousy from that lunch with the joint had never abated. Everything about Suzana had begun to annoy him. Her habit of kissing him without brushing her teeth, the funk of her hairy armpits, the panties scattered about the floor, the Fagner records, and the roach cemetery that made the place stink so badly of patchouli and cannabis that the building manager had come to complain. The apartment had become a meeting place for dubious sorts, a coming and going of weirdos that made him envy Lana Ley's eviction. He followed Lana's example and kicked her out. Later he regretted it.

Ribeiro didn't know there was such a thing as subjectivity. He had no sense of humor. He was dumb, and a faithful friend. He died an eternal adolescent, survived by no children or wife, more of a cousin than uncle to his sister's son. His mother had died young of heart problems, and Celeste had stepped into her shoes. He had only a few memories of his mother, of her big eyes, of being bowled over by the surf and being saved by her hands, nothing more. His father was a taciturn military man from the state of Sergipe, who longed to see his son graduate from Agulhas Negras Military Academy, rising to ranks well above his own. He never hid his frustration at his son's performance at school, and spoke of his disillusionment to friends and relatives. Ribeiro didn't rely on him; he only trusted his sister, just her—she was support, solace, home.

The beach was his reason for being. With every pink sunset, with every storm or full-moon night, he confirmed that he had made the right choice. Ribeiro didn't go to university and finished his studies at a bad public high school, but he managed to make a living from the geography that he worshiped. The minute he graduated from high school, he worked hard to obtain a lifeguard certificate and got a job as a swimming instructor at Lifeguard Post Six. He didn't make much, but it was enough to get his father off his back. Apart from that, he seduced the virgins who passed the bikini test. Unlike Sílvio, he didn't do it out of perversion, he was sincere. Ribeiro never saw his fetish as a sin, much less a fetish—it was true love. He grew old without realizing it. His age was a trump card for a good while, until his shelf life expired.

When he had just turned fifty, he got a job at Impact, a gym on the way up to the favela Ladeira dos Tabajaras. Impact prepared thighs and triceps for Carnival, that was its forte. The muses Marinara, Monique, and Marininha had all trained there. The instructors sold steroids and the brawn shot up in the bathroom. Ribeiro hated being in that environment, but he had no choice. He could only make a living teaching Schwarzenegger disciples. He existed in a state of bewilderment. The girls no longer wanted to be like the bombshells Leila, Danuza, Florinda, and Norma—not Sílvio's Norma, but Norma Bengell.

Ribeiro had discovered Norma Bengell as a teenager. A bohemian uncle had had a fling with a cabaret dancer and smuggled his nephew into the wings of a Carlos Machado production. Ribeiro watched, live, as Norma parodied Bardot. He was sixteen. He jerked off to the end of his days to that image. He memorized it down to the last detail. Memories of his mother mingled with those of the muse.

Women had lost their appeal, they had ceased to be women, he used to say. Why so much muscle? Few of them turned Ribeiro on, the conversation didn't flow, it was all very boring. Worse, they all treated him as if he were harmless. Then Lucíola came along. He gave her the first set of exercises, but she was new and couldn't keep up with everyone else during Jair's squats. "Row, row!" yelled Ribeiro in encouragement, but it was no use. He gave her some water and suggested private lessons. Lucíola might injure herself if she tried to keep up with the group. He offered his services outside of the gym, the beach being the most appropriate place. She took him up on his offer. She really wouldn't have survived at Impact for very long.

They met one splendid morning at the fish market and began their walk toward Leme. She was pretty, very pretty, beautiful, in fact, Ribeiro only noticed there. Her red cheeks contrasted with her white skin and her delicate face was marked by thick, black eyebrows that gave her features a masculine touch. By the time they got to Lifeguard Post One, they were in love. Her father couldn't find out, he was very strict, and Lucíola was still a virgin. Perhaps she was afraid that her first time might be with some brute, it's hard to say, but Ribeiro was exactly what she wanted. Hypnotized by the possibility of taking her virginity, he played his cards skillfully and slowly until one day, after a lesson, Lucíola cut her foot on a shard of glass and he carried her to his apartment to bandage it up. It took less than a fraction of a second for his hand to forget the cut and slip between her legs. Lucíola was quiet and Ribeiro did what he had to. Afterwards, he left her on the corner near her apartment and went home to remember.

Sometime around midnight, the deflowerer woke with a start to the sound of someone banging on the door. He ran to look through the peephole. An older man, accompanied by a well-built young man, stared at him through the hole. It was Lucíola's father and he wanted to talk. He had barely turned the key in the lock when he was hit in the face by the door. The young man followed up with a sequence of punches and kicks, while calling him a dirty old man. It was Lucíola's brother, he found out later. It was the first time Ribeiro had been called an old man. The whole thing lasted five minutes—not even that—but it felt endless. When they grew tired, the father told the shitty little gym instructor that he was dead if he ever went anywhere near his daughter again. And he disappeared, dragging his troglodyte son behind him. Ribeiro suffered a lot, a mixture of humiliation and missing her. You didn't fuck a virgin only once. The first time didn't even count; the secret was how the plot developed, the discoveries, the way they gradually loosened up. "Then it actually gets a bit boring," he would say. Lucíola remained a dream, leaving him with an awareness of his age and a sense of the ridiculous, to boot.

Bye-bye, young ladies, it was time to move on. He tried twenty-nine-year-olds, thirty-one-year-olds, thirty-two, thirty-three, all complex and demanding pains in the ass. Virgins were like him: simple. They dreamed of gentle sex and that was all. What could be better than that? And Ribeiro knew how to detect problems, abort missions, give up on the ones who didn't relax after two weeks. By the time he was in his forties, he'd grown tired of the missionary position. That's why Suzana had driven him wild, because she was the perfect combination of naivety and call girl. She got him all flustered with the obscenities she proposed, without losing her childish air. Lucíola was the end of the road, the last virgin to love him, his last attempt to go back to being himself. Suzana was the furthest he'd been from himself, the only one with whom he had shared a roof, the closest thing to a wife he'd had. Thirty-three years after the incident in the garden with the ferns, Ribeiro was still consumed with jealousy. Sílvio shouldn't have done what he did.

The coffin was lowered into the grave without tears or words of praise for the deceased. Inácio stood there, pallid and unfazed. Burn in hell, he muttered. The gravediggers slathered cement over the grave with shovels, giving the ceremony an odd aura reminiscent of a bathroom renovation. The group left, single file, with the transvestite in front, weaving her way around tombstones to the main path. Ribeiro pretended to follow the group, but turned left and found himself a remote vantage point, hidden among the head-stones. He watched over the grave, certain she would come, alone, after everyone else, to mourn her lover. He imagined Suzana's gaze; finally, he would know the truth. When he was kicked out by the guards, it was already late at night. Suzana hadn't come. Maybe he'd been wrong after all. He had suffered for nothing. Outside the cemetery, with his back to the fence, admiring the lights in the favela of Dona Marta, he understood: he didn't love Suzana, he never had. In his jealous delirium, she had cheated on him with Sílvio and would reappear there to put an end to his uncertainty. But she hadn't held up her end of the bargain. She had nothing in common with him, or his friends. She was a stranger, an excuse not to think about Ruth.

Staring at the lights on the hillside, Ribeiro bid his torment farewell. He lived the last four years of his life without passion, fervor, jealousy, or rancor. He was cured. It was good and bad, because in a way he was already dead. He had died there, outside the cemetery.

RIBEIRO

* September 4, 1933
† November 13, 2013

"HEY, SAMPAIO, you got the blues?"

"I have indeed, Ribeiro, but there are only three packets in stock. I suggest you take them because I don't know when the next lot will be delivered."

What would I be without my personal pharmacist?

"I'll take the lot."

Viagra is as revolutionary as the pill, but no one has the courage to say so. And with this business of having to use condoms, well, a man needs a little help. Then someone goes and invents this miracle, on sale in any decent drugstore, and without a prescription if you know Sampaio! It's freedom! I can't imagine life without it anymore.

I didn't see age creep up on me, that sly bastard. At thirty, you don't look fifteen anymore; at forty, the last signs of your twenties disappear; at fifty, your thirties. It takes a decade or so to lose things. I didn't notice, I felt the same, full of energy, mature, on top of my game. It was only when Suzana and I broke up that it hit me. I'd lived with her for over a year, convinced she was having an affair with Sílvio, and I let myself go to seed. I stopped weighing myself, measuring my waistline, biceps, I went off-diet, didn't sleep much, drank more than usual, and tried some other shit. Suzana's fault, it was all her fault.

The morning I came home a wreck after the scene I'd made, playing the betrayed husband, I opened the door with a bleeding knee and Sílvio's laughter still echoing in my head. I undressed, hurried to the bathroom, and accidentally caught sight of my reflection out of the corner of my eye. There I was, buck naked, in the mirror. I was an old man. Shocked, I went closer to investigate. Gray hair, bags under my eyes, sagging cheeks, flaccid neck, double chin. My nipples were bigger, my stomach was swelling, a gut beginning to form. My cock was average and my arms and legs still had muscles but were showing obvious signs of decline. My well-being was based on simple, routine things. Taking them away from me, as Suzana had done, had upset a delicate balance. My mother's smile, being knocked over by the wave, her hands, Suzana's mouth, her easy laughter, me being an orphan. I sat on the toilet and cried, then I phoned Celeste.

Carlos helped a lot. He was taking volleyball seriously and my sister had me coach him. He cured me of my depression. Him and Frank Sinatra. I've never been to America. It was my dream to visit America. My Sinatra collection won me a lot of women back in the day. These days I hide it so it won't scare them off.

"Send it down the back, down the back! . . . Attaboy! What a comeback! Seventeen to fifteen! It's the triumph of experience."

I arranged a game on the beach with Carlos, a best of three with his son and a pal from college. These kids haven't even got hair on their bodies and they think they're going to beat the lion here.

"The bump, the precise set, the indefensible spike. Go on, kneel down, you don't have the moves! Must be the crap you eat."

I'm tired.

I woke up early to teach a lesson to seniors. Some old girls who roasted in the sun all their lives and now they're like vampires, can't even see light. Melanoma's a bitch. I've had a few moles removed myself. I don't like sunscreen.

It's hard to accept that those old women were fifteen once. Now they all have to get up before dawn, but it's not like they're missing any sleep. Better to have something to do. They complain of insomnia a lot. They complain a lot, period. And who's the hero who gets up before dawn to meet a bunch of seventy-year-old zombies? Ribeiro here. But it's good because by nine o'clock half my workday is over. I play a game of beach volleyball, nap until about four, then go meet the beach crowd again to see what life has in store.

It hasn't had much lately, but today looks promising.

I was going to say no to the old ladies. I went to the building where they all live, on Rua República do Peru, to tell them I couldn't do it. But the niece of the one in 401 came down to say her aunt wasn't feeling well. Fifty-seven, fifty-eight-ish, nice figure, long hair, tight jeans. When I saw her I changed my mind. I said I'd come to find out what their objectives were, ad-libbed it for about a quarter of an hour, and suggested I pay them each a visit to get to know them better. I suffered through those eleven floors. Time is cruel to women. I left the one with the niece for last.

The aunt was asleep in her bedroom.

I suggested she install grab bars in the bathroom and asked a few harmless questions: if she lived there, if she was just visiting. Alda had just split with her husband and didn't want to live with her mother. She thanked me for my interest and praised me, saying I was a very considerate teacher. I asked her out on a date. She said she left the shop at six. Bingo!

It feels good to swim in the cold water off Copacabana. That warm piss soup in the Northeast of the country is disgusting. But the water here is dirty, the current's changed direction, no one's brave enough to go for a dip. Oily brown foam. One of the advantages of age is that you stop caring about the distant future. Now I just sit on the sand with the pigeons and risk skin cancer—I ain't about to slop on sunscreen. Check out the goddesses walking past—my God, they still exist. Not for me, not anymore, never again. I've had to come to terms with whores and good girls over fifty. Neurotic, all of them, like Alda in 401. I can tell she's desperate.

—

"Bye, Carlos, tell your mom I'll stop by tomorrow. I'm meeting someone. Yep, the lion here ain't dead! Don't worry, I won't ruin the family name, I've been to see Sampaio!"

I never wanted to have children. My nephew was the closest I ever got, with the advantage of being able to give him back to my sister whenever we hit a glitch. All men become slaves to their kid's moms, even after they're divorced. I never found a mother, not for me or my kids. I thought about getting a vasectomy, but I was afraid it might affect my ability to get it up.

The water in these beach showers is straight from the sewers. So what? It feels good to wash off the salt! Álvaro drinks water from the tap and he's still alive.

"Hey, where's my coconut water? Could you pass me my fanny pack? It's behind the counter there."

I've known this guy since he was a kid. Now he's inherited his dad's kiosk. Where's my pill? Here! The Niagara-blue diamond.

* * *

After the beating I got from Lucíola's father, and the phrase "dirty old man" her brother left as a memento, I decided to become a monk—I gave up smoking, became chaste. I was ashamed to approach girls, afraid of hearing a "no." I felt like an idiot and stopped taking the risk. I'd wake up before dawn, run the beach end to end, coach Carlos, and swim in the afternoon when I was done teaching. I became a machine, an Adonis with no libido. I didn't feel like it and had no idea what was going to become of me. All Álvaro could talk about was his inability to get it up, so I avoided him. Sílvio had ditched the gang to go live on the wild side, Neto was married, and Ciro had just died. I practically married my sister.

Celeste was very practical. She had decided to try life on her own. She still liked her husband but wanted to leave him. She was pretty brave; at a time when most women are scared witless of losing their partners, Celeste came out with this one. It was good, because I didn't have to tiptoe around my sister's apartment and I was a male presence there while she was between relationships. I slept at my place but spent the day at hers, and we were happy like that. It didn't last. Celeste started seeing a production engineer who'd started at her firm. I asked what a production engineer did, but Celeste wasn't sure. "Something to do with planning, I don't know, one day you can ask him," she said. I didn't. I was insanely jealous of the guy. I hadn't had sex for a year, I was tense, and I got it in my head that Carlos shouldn't be left alone, so I started waiting for Celeste in the living room with a scowl on my face. The minute she turned the key in the lock I'd start in with the interrogation, wanting to know where she'd been, who she'd been with, if she'd eaten. At first she thought it was cute. She said I was bonkers and would shoo me out, but when I started getting aggressive, she was frank with me. With a straight face, she told me to go get laid. "The first one you see, Ribeiro, just do it; don't think about it, then tell me how it was," she said. And she banned me from her apartment after seven at night.

As if it wasn't enough, Neto passed away.

Ciro used to try and help Álvaro by reassuring him that all men have their bad days, except me. Not anymore. When Celeste told me to get back in the game after a long sabbatical, I, frightened by how short life is, picked up where I'd left off. I didn't want the ones who were interested in me even if they were the last women alive, and the ones I was interested in didn't want me under any circumstance. Young women were now standoffish, and turned their noses up at me. Solange was the best of a bad lot.

We met in my dentist's elevator. She worked in an accountant's office in the same building on Rua Figueiredo de Magalhães. I'd just had my teeth cleaned and my mouth was sparkling, which must have helped. She was short and bug-eyed, with dyed red hair, but overall she was okay. We went to La Mole. She had the escalope with Piedmontese rice and I had the breaded shrimp. We had wine, ice cream, coffee, and devoured the petits fours. During dinner, Solange confessed that she was saving up for a boob job. Is there something wrong with her breasts? I wondered. I don't mind if they're small; I actually like them like that, as long as they're not saggy. We took a taxi to Catete and got out in front of her building. Solange was wide open. I was already on the third step, with my foot in the foyer, when a thought struck me. What if I can't get it up? Cold sweat began streaming down my neck that very second. Solange hadn't noticed yet, so I pretended everything was fine, wished her good night with cinematic flair, asked her out on a second date, kissed her hand, and took off. I didn't want her to think I was insecure. Nothing scares off the opposite sex more than that.

Sampaio sold energy drinks, imported vitamins, I liked him. Once when I came down with a bad flu, he gave me an antibiotics injection that put me on my feet again in just one day. He became my GP. Sampaio was very discreet. If he mentioned Viagra, it was by its biblical name: sildenafil. Tadalafil, for Cialis, and vardenafil, for Levitra, had yet to be invented. I didn't sleep a wink the night before my first time with Solange, imagining myself trying to have sex but not being able to. I dreamed her pussy was a bronze statue. At daybreak I went out to buy sedatives. I'd survived the end of my relationship with Suzana on Lexotan prescribed by Sampaio. I was grateful to him. I arrived early, he was late. When he saw me at the counter with bags under my eyes, he asked if someone else had died. I begged him for tranquilizers. He eyed me suspiciously.

"Tranquilizers for what? Do you want to relax?"

"More or less," I said, head down.

"Sorry to pry, Ribeiro, but what's the problem?"

"My sister's seeing someone . . ."

"Uh-huh . . ."

"She told me to get back in the game . . . "

"I see . . . "

"I'm going out for dinner, tonight, and I think there might be dessert."

"Say no more," he said, and dragged me off to the back of the pharmacy to the cubicle where they gave injections. Sampaio closed the curtain and took the blood pressure monitor down from the wall.

"Do you have a history of high blood pressure?"

"No," I said.

I forgot to mention my mother's heart attack, nor did he ask. He just pumped the air, staring at the monitor with a serious face.

"One hundred twenty over seventy, no danger," he said, and disappeared into the stock room.

He returned quickly holding a packet.

"Ribeiro, the only reason I don't compare this wonder to the Lord Jesus Christ is because it's a capital sin. But it is, Ribeiro, this here is the Lord Jesus Christ."

I took the packet. Viagra, said the label.

"I suggest you take it about three hours ahead of time so you don't have any surprises and are already fired up by the time you get there."

"Have you tried it?" I asked.

"Yes," he said. "When it first came, and I haven't stopped since."

The same thing happened to me.

I gave it to Solange like a jackhammer. It wasn't enough. Viagra separated sex and love. As a lover, I was jealous, stupid and needy. Sildenafil suppressed my romantic expectations and I fell into temptation. Sílvio would have been proud of me. I fucked like a gymnast, spent money I didn't have on the twenty-year-olds in the dives on Avenida Prado Júnior, and grew fond of the disposable robes at the Centauro, where I almost went bankrupt after two hookers locked themselves in one of the little rooms with me. They started half-heartedly, not making much of an effort, but when it was almost time to turn the red light back on, which signaled the end of the session, the harlots started rubbing each other like octopuses. It gave me a huge boner and I asked for another session. And another and another. When it was time to pay they explained that with the two of them, everything was double. I left without a dime and had to borrow money from Celeste. I said it was for a root canal.

I put a pill in my mouth and swallow. Alda, here I come. It's been ages since I've had a decent woman. It'll be good for a change.

"How much is this? And how much is on my tab? Then let's settle up; I don't like to be in debt."

I ran into Álvaro yesterday on Rua Francisco Sá. I was leaving Sampaio's pharmacy and came face-to-face with him. We hadn't seen each other for several years, since Neto's funeral, I guess. Boy is he in bad shape, and his head's a mess. He called me Ciro about three times and stumbled another ten. I tried to give him a hand but he got offended. I was too embarrassed to ask if it was ischemia.

Copacabana has changed a lot—it's these buses churning out black smoke. I'll have a beer, thanks. I love a dive. I like to watch the drunks.

Álvaro insists that Sílvio died in Lapa, but he's wrong. It was in Cinelândia, in front of the Bola Preta Carnival bloc headquarters. I went to the funeral, Álvaro! The disagreement was threatening to turn into a fight so I cut him off.

"Forget it," I said. "What difference does it make? Sílvio lied; he said he was going to Porto Alegre but he wound up in Niterói and never called again. Remember how he used to snort? Bad breath, smoking, talking nonstop? He's gone, and good riddance."

Álvaro thought that was funny. We said we'd get together one of these days. Who knows? I miss the gang. Álvaro, Neto, Sílvio, and Ciro.

I was crazy about Ciro. Ciro was the best of us. We had his leftovers. Women could sense Ciro's presence even with their backs turned. By his smell. When he walked into a room, they'd all turn around like robots. The married ones, the single ones, fiancées, debutants. And Ciro was a fun winner, full of stories. He knew his politics, he was intelligent, a compulsive reader, romantic, and he was even good on the guitar. No one could hold a candle to him. We joked that he was the shark and we were the pilot fish. Truth be told, we fought as hard for his attention as the ladies did.

He spent his holidays in Búzios, in a fisherman's cottage. The most coveted beauty of Ipanema drove her VW for four hours through the night just to meet him in paradise. When she got there, Ciro said he was going to fetch supper and dove into the sea holding a knife. He came back with a live lobster. After the meal, they jumped into bed and the lucky woman spread the crustacean hunter myth around Rio. To ensure that his number was always a success, Ciro started leaving a crate of the creatures tied up on the ocean floor. Whenever a candidate showed up—and one always would, because there was a queue—he'd emerge from the waves holding the lobster.

We loved Ciro.

I was there, beside him, the day he met Ruth. We arrived at Juliano's party together, ready for yet another unforgettable night. Sílvio brought the arsenal and Álvaro and Neto met us at the door as planned. The women all turned to look as Ciro walked in and we tried to figure out what would be left for the picking, but one of them didn't turn around. Ruth. She didn't even notice we were there. She laughed out loud, in a circle of guests gathered around someone playing the guitar, and went on singing that song . . . *Today, I want the most beautiful of roses* . . . "A Noite do Meu Bem" by Dolores Duran. She had the voice of a nightclub singer—low, sensual—and she sure was something to look at. The whole room stopped to listen. I was crazy about Ruth; it was love at first sight. When I glanced sideways, I realized the same thing had happened to Ciro. I'd never seen him like that. Ciro took the lead, walked over to the group, asked for the guitar, and began to play a beautiful song by Vinicius de Moraes that Odete Lara used to sing . . . *Without you, my love . . . I am no one . . .* Ruth took the female voice, Ciro, the male voice, and they finished together, to a standing ovation, forever in love.

My world fell apart.

How could I compete? They disappeared together and someone started playing "Lígia." "Lígia," the soundtrack of my heartache. I listened to "Lígia" many times, thinking about her, thinking about Ciro. It was hard to go out with them, see them so happy together. Ruth wasn't a girl anymore, but so what? If she'd chosen me, I'd have had children with her, a family. I'd have given up cradle-snatching once and for all. I'd have been hers alone. But she chose Ciro, of course she chose Ciro. Heck, *I'd* have chosen Ciro. But I would have looked after her. I'd never have done what he did, the abominable thing he did to her.

That's why I threw myself into Suzana. That's why I can't forgive Sílvio, because I loved Ruth my whole life but never overstepped the mark. I watched Ciro make her happy, *really* happy, and then kill her, lock her away, spit on her. Serves you right, Ciro. That cancer served you right.

—

This is a strong one. I'm sweating. Think about Alda. Damn traffic. Lycra clothes, my God, the world's gone crazy. Women dress like whores even to go to the corner store. Check out the ass on that one! Vacuum-sealed in those leggings. I learned what leggings were at the gym.

I'm a bit dizzy when I get to my building. I stop in the foyer to catch my breath. The doorman notices and asks if he can help. "I'm fine," I say, feeling Álvaro's irritation. Then I think I was rude for no reason. I ask if there's any post, but before he checks he says I'm red. "It's the muggy weather," I say. But it isn't muggy, it's cool, in fact. "What, they're going to turn off the water in the building? Now? No, wait for me to have a shower. Tell them I'm going up, stall them for me!" I drag myself to the elevator. The building hasn't incinerated its trash for thirty years, but the smell's still here. First floor . . . second . . . this elevator's going to fall. Fifth . . . sixth, my floor. The neighbor in 610 is cooking beans. She cooks beans every day. The corridor reeks. I can't stand beans. I feel so queasy. Where's the key? This stench is going to kill me.

My sanctuary. Quick, to the shower. Whoa . . . black ceiling, what's up, lion? Put your head down, breathe deeply. It's getting better. Migraine coming on. I'll take my swimming trunks off in the shower so I don't get sand everywhere. Boy, does it take a long time for this piece of junk to heat up. I'm going to get an electric one. Electric showers have come a long way. It's getting warmer . . . C'mon, for chrissake, they're going to turn off the water soon. It's warm. Thank God. I'm actually sweating in the water. I think I'm going to throw up. Now it's boiling, goddamn, pain-in-the-ass shower.

When I reach for the cold faucet, I feel the tingling creep up from my right hand, through my arm and into my chest. My chest. It tightens, as if a giant is crushing me with his fingers. A stabbing pain in my plexus. My lungs are paralyzed, my jaw locks, and I'm short of breath. I try to stay calm and think about calling the doorman, the police. What's Celeste's phone number? 97 . . . 9756 . . . 753 . . . 75 . . . I try to remember. I get out of the shower holding onto the curtain, the plastic can't take my weight, and I kiss the canvas. I feel better than I did standing up. Lie down, put your legs up. The floor's cold as hell. Another stabbing pain, I don't believe it. Relax, lion. God, I can't see a thing. Cough, I heard on TV that you have to cough if you think you're having a heart attack. I'm having a heart attack. I can't cough if I'm asphyxiating like this.

I need to find Carlos. He'll come with his son . . . what's his name? It doesn't matter. Carlos will drag me to a taxi, take me to an ER . . . Where's my cell? I left it in the living room. I'm screwed. I'm not getting up from here. My heart's going to leap out of my mouth. Here it comes, here it comes . . . here it comes . . . there . . . it goes.

It's okay, Ribeiro. You're not going to have a stroke, Alzheimer's, or Parkinson's. You won't be pushed around in a wheelchair by an ugly nurse, you won't drool like Álvaro or come out of a hospital full of holes like Ciro. You're a lucky guy. That's the last of the water. This is it. Is this it? Yep, this is it. I shouldn't have taken that pill on an empty stomach. Forget the empty stomach, it was going to happen anyway. I was taking four or five a week. Viagra gave me ten extra years of service life. It's fair. More than fair. I'd trade the next ten for the last seven. Long live the troupe at the Centauro, the trannies at The Pussery, Erotika, and internet sex. I lived it up. Now it's over.

I didn't live at all. None of it was worth Ruth.

I went to see her at her sister's place, some ten years after she got divorced. She'd become distant and bitter. When she saw me, she cursed us all: Sílvio, Neto, Álvaro, and me. She didn't mention Ciro. She couldn't, she didn't have it in her. I'd gone there hoping to tell her how I felt, to propose something or other, whatever she wanted, but I didn't have the courage. She asked how the mob was. Like that, the "mob" . . . . I said I hadn't seen them for a while. That was shortly after the beating I got because of Lucíola, when I tried to change my ways and find myself a real woman. Ruth asked me to leave. She said we were all dead to her and went into the bedroom without saying goodbye. Her sister saw me to the door and made me promise not to come back. Ciro had left nothing of the old Ruth. Selfish bastard. He always was.

I stopped making plans. The future ended there.

From then on, I accepted that I'd have to screw older gals who were further and further removed from what I wanted. Like Alda, who I made out to be a Miss Universe but who is really the bottom of the pit. Sorry, Alda, I won't be seeing you later.

ALDA WAITED for Ribeiro at the door of her work for over an hour. She went home humiliated, rejected by an old man. The next day, the news traveled through the building: the instructor hadn't shown up for the six o'clock lesson or volleyball at ten. Carlos called his apartment and rang the doorbell, and the doorman managed to break down the door. They found Ribeiro lying in the flooded bathroom. The building's water had come back on, and the shower had overflowed. Ribeiro's stiff body, beginning to decompose, wasn't a pleasant sight. Carlos called a hearse, tried to dry the floor with a bath towel, and phoned Celeste to tell her what had happened. Alda smiled unintentionally. She didn't wish for anyone's demise, but her relief at not having been rejected by a man in his seventies was greater than any sense of loss. And she thought it romantic that she had been the old-timer from Copacabana's last chance at love. It had a certain charm. She went to the cemetery to pay her respects.

Burials were a thing of the past. With the inauguration of the crematorium at São Francisco Xavier Cemetery, families had begun to prefer ashes to bones. Celeste took charge of the preparations. Her men helped her a lot, but she insisted on seeing to the details herself, ordering the wreaths, choosing her brother's coffin and suit. Carlos covered his uncle with the Botafogo Football Club flag and placed the volleyball from his last game in his hands. He gave the speech. He was sincere and affectionate. His mother didn't want to speak, but she held on to her son, nodding with approval at the end of his sentences. She was the one who gave the order for the oven to be switched on. A mournful melody played as the coffin passed over the conveyor belt of metal rollers and disappeared into a low, dark tunnel, like suitcases in an airport x-ray machine. The final product wasn't released until the following day. At the front desk, Celeste showed them her piece of paper with a number on it, was given the box, and drove with it to Leme Rock. My brother loved the beach, she said, revealing the contents of the urn among the fishermen, rods, and hooks. Carlos and his son each took a handful of their uncle, Celeste did the same, and the three of them threw Ribeiro into the wind, repeating the gesture until there was nothing left. He hovered around the family, before being sucked up with the vultures in a rising current. A few particles brushed the faces of those witnessing the ceremony. No one complained. The fishermen were respectful of the family's rite, although they were still nauseated by the cloud of organic dust.

Celeste had her feet planted firmly on the ground; she saw as much greatness in death as she did in life. Girls develop quickly and, without her mother, Celeste had had to grow up fast. Woman of the house, wife to her father, mother to her brother. It saddened her deeply to say goodbye to Ribeiro, but not so much that she didn't feel proud of her grown son, her healthy grandson, the good men she had in her life. She had lived alone for a long time, but her grandson had taken the place of her son, and her new love the place of the old one, such that she had never experienced the emptiness of her losses. She didn't have the temperament for that. She had always lived surrounded by people; she didn't believe in loneliness. Ribeiro hadn't been well—he'd lost the innocence he'd maintained for so long. She'd preferred to see him dispersed in the atmosphere rather than roaming Copacabana, spending money on whores, taking stimulants, at risk of being beaten up, mugged, or arrested. It's good that he's stopped now, she thought, as she buttoned up her black dress.

It was the first time Álvaro had been to a cremation. He thought it was deplorable and undignified to shove a dead man into an ash factory, mixed with the remains of other dead people. No one cleans that thing. Ribeiro's sister's calm shocked Álvaro, his last friend left alive. Celeste should have hidden her acceptance better. She was crying, it was true, but smiling, smiling enough that you could see her teeth; it wasn't right. Her son and grandson were more discreet, her ex and current partner, too. "Women are all attention seekers," he told himself, in his incorrigible misogyny. Álvaro had hoped to see someone agonizing over his friend's death, but everyone seemed resigned, including him. It bothered him that he was the last man standing, with a one-hundred-percent chance of being next. In addition, he was bored. Was it the fault of the ceremony or the heat? Why did the weather always get muggy when someone died? Feeling short of breath, he sat at the back of the small audience. He listened to Carlos, and thought it was a beautiful speech, but was shocked at how naturally those in attendance were acting. There was nothing natural about death. The anger, the helplessness, and the mourning of times past were missing. The heartbreak was missing.

RUTH WAS THE GODDESS OSHUN; she was Mary and Magdalene, the consummate woman—she always had been. Pride of her father, mirror of her mother, she was marriage material. She'd have been happy at any time, era, or place; she'd have suited a merchant or a warrior. She was Aphrodite incarnate, the embodiment of femininity. Future exemplary wife, she came of age in the heyday of the late 1950s, to the elegant soundtrack of Tom Jobim and Vinicius de Moraes. Love was the order of the day and adults drank away their sorrows. Ruth yearned for her own day to come. She was a prize and knew it—she was saving herself for Mr. Right. She nurtured a childish romanticism while fulfilling the requirements of the new era.

She was one of the first to know what it was to be free to drink and smoke, to sing at parties, to wear a bikini, to be courted, and to laugh without being vulgar. She was cultured and intelligent—she wouldn't have been complete if she wasn't. She read Nietzsche and crocheted. Her education at Colégio Sion had suppressed any excesses; she was just the right degree of easygoing, and restrained in equal measure. A nice girl. Her friends turned out to be much more brazen. Unlike Ruth, they had no choice. At the beginning of the sexual revolution, with the contraceptive pill, they were pioneers in the art of having sex without questioning whether or not it was worth it. But not Ruth. She waited patiently. And while she did, she listened to Dolores Duran.

She was still a virgin when she enrolled in university to study language and literature. The young men quickly noticed her graceful walk, broad smile, beautiful voice, and the way she put her hands on her hips when she danced samba. Ruth paraded across campus, high on the daily contact with testosterone. In response to the stimuli her hair grew thick, her skin rosy, and her nipples were permanently erect. Everything about her ripened as she waited for a moment that never arrived. She read Plato's *Symposium* with her study group and discovered that she was androgynous. Some terrible god had cut her original body in two, separating her from her male half. She wanted to find him, get him back. At night, she fantasized about being sewn back together, stitch by stitch, skin on skin. A shiver would run through her and she would fall asleep aroused. But Ruth forgot to heed the wise man's warning: "We only love what we don't have."

Sérgio was a sensitive, serious, attentive young man. He was studying philosophy and wanted to be a teacher. Her friends were rooting for Beto, the Alain Delon of economics, but Ruth preferred Sérgio, with whom she had discovered *Symposium*. Virginity was still the norm, but it was no longer compulsory. Her more progressive friends urged her to go for it and, exasperated by her reserve, called her a prude.

Her libido was threatening to burst the dike. Ruth thought about love day and night. Politics, war, Cuba, the future, and the nuclear bomb were of little interest to her. She decided it would be with Sérgio. She agreed to finish a project with him at his place and, one sunny afternoon in the spring of 1962, she lay on his bed and, with a kiss, made the invitation. Caught by surprise, Sérgio applied himself to the mission. He was shy, and tried to hide his lack of experience. He was respectful, technical, and amateur. Ruth left his room with the uneasy impression that she hadn't changed. She was still chaste. The frustration made her balk, preserve herself even more. If she kept trying, she thought, she might not feel the impact of the big event. Sérgio had taken her hymen, that was certain, but he hadn't even touched her restlessness. It is passion that deflowers a woman, awakens her senses: smell, touch, taste, sight, a tingling in her ears. Ruth was still virginal. Who was going to rescue her?

It was Ciro; Aristophanes had been talking about Ciro.

It was chance that brought them together, at Irene's cousin's birthday; Irene and Ruth were the best of friends. Juliano had noticed that his cousin's friends were ripe for the picking and had organized for them to come to the sing-along. That's why Ruth was there when Ciro, Neto, Álvaro, Ribeiro, and Sílvio walked into the room. She could just as easily not have been, but she was. But even if she wasn't, Ciro and Ruth would have met one day, somehow. It was destined to be.

Today I want the most beautiful of roses

Everyone stopped talking to listen when Ruth sang. She did more than just sing, she made the song hers. The long hours spent beside the record player, the vinyl worn from being played over and over, her crystal-clear understanding of the lyrics, her identification with the sorrow of the song, her husky voice, all of it really did make one want to stop and pay attention. Near the end, when the protagonist confesses that because her love has been so long in the making, perhaps her gaze is no longer as pure as she would like it to be, Ruth looked at the people listening and saw Ciro standing at the back of the room. The floor gave way, the wall receded, and the image of the handsome man loomed, giant and glowing, before her. Her head span. She felt the blood race in her veins while her arteries constricted. The rush of hormones gave her goose bumps and a knot in the stomach, and her heart beat faster. Her poisoning began there. She finished the song to much applause and pretended to be calm, smiling and doing her best to control the whirlwind inside her, until she saw out of the corner of her eye that Ciro was approaching. She shook from head to foot. He took a guitar from the hands of one of the serenaders, sat in front of Ruth, and, without taking his eyes off her, played the first few chords of a song and sang.

Without you, I have no reason

"Samba em Prelúdio." Ruth blushed, everyone noticed. Ciro smiled, he was irresistible. With a nod, he invited the muse to accompany him in a duet. She accepted the challenge. They sailed through the notes, savoring the poet's words.

Without you, my love, I am no one

There was no pause. When the song was over, Ciro returned the guitar to its owner and stood while the audience applauded. Then he shouted that Ruth was his and dragged her away from the rabble. Despite their resentment, none of the other guests dared contradict the hero. Absolute lord of the scene, Ciro swept up the queen with the skill of Eros. Many couples were formed that night after witnessing their meeting.

Ciro's hand squeezing hers—the calm it brought her. She couldn't remember a thing, just fumbling with buttons and pressing her face against the skin of a man she didn't know. She stayed there like that, eyes closed, breathing the same air as him, listening to the rhythmic beating of his heart. She wanted to be sewn to him forever. His large hands clasped her face and she dared look up. Ciro brought his mouth to hers and opened it with his lips, teeth, tongue. Ruth wrapped her arms around his neck and felt the roughness of his beard, took in his manly smell, the cigarettes. There's nothing ethereal about love. It's flesh, it's physical, it's brutal. Ciro ran his hands up Ruth's legs and, without questioning whether he should or not, slid his fingers inside her. The gesture put her on guard. For the first time since she'd set eyes on him, she began to ask questions. Who is he? she thought, firmly holding the intrusive hand. Ciro understood. He was also reflecting, for the first time, about what had happened since the moment he saw her.

"My name's Ciro, I have a law degree, and this has never happened to me before."

It was what he could say. It wasn't a trick; how to make her understand? Ciro was on unfamiliar terrain, but his sincere reply had the desired effect. Ruth accepted his innocence and consented.

Someone appeared on the veranda and hurried along things that were asking to be hurried along. They left without saying goodbye to anyone. In the hall outside the apartment, Ciro pressed the elevator button insistently while Ruth stared at the floorboards. She wasn't going to his place and he couldn't go to hers; there was nowhere, so it would have to be there. They counted the seconds with serious expressions on their faces. Anyone looking at them would have sworn they'd just quarreled. When they stepped into the mirrored cubicle, Ciro waited to ascend two floors and pressed the emergency button. The door opened, showing an ugly slab of concrete. Ruth kept still. He held her against the wall with a deep kiss and everything spun again. Exploring her breasts and belly, Ciro knelt, lifting Ruth's skirt up to her navel, then pressed his face into her and inhaled.

"My name's Ruth," she said.

Ciro stood to admire her. His hands slid up to the back of her neck, and she wrapped her legs around him. He unfastened his belt hastily and looked at her again. Now serious, he held her by the hips and forced himself inside her. It was done. Someone bellowed down the shaft for them to stop holding up the elevator. There was no time. He positioned her in the corner of the tiny square and violated her until he was finished. Ruth was no longer a virgin. She had found her reason for being.

"I saw Jesus," she told her friends.

She liked President Goulart because Ciro liked President Goulart, Che Guevara, Bob Dylan, and Noel Rosa. Ruth was Ciro's first lady, his Jackie, she played the perfect hostess for her beloved. She took an interest in politics again, debated the bomb, became friends with Célia, married Irene to Álvaro, laughed at Sílvio's excesses, and never understood why Ribeiro was eternally single. She felt sorry for him, but didn't know why. She fell in love with everything that orbited around her sun. They marched against the coup of 1964, watched the musical *Opinião*, starring Nara Leão and later Maria Bethânia, paraded with the Banda de Ipanema Carnival block, went to the beach, and loved each other like crazy. Their honeymoon was in Búzios. Ciro took her to hunt for that night's lobster. They dived among the rocks and fucked on the sand, on the quay, in the bedroom, in the other rooms. Ruth had only known orgasms in her dreams, and Ciro made them real. He was a pioneer.

But it is precisely here, at the apex of romantic realization, that a woman's fate is sealed. Drunk on love, Ruth was no longer herself. She was Ciro, she was their son, the house, the couple. She said she was complete. She had forgotten the philosopher's warning. She never suspected that those ten years of happiness were just the opening act to Tosca, the accumulation of everything that she wouldn't have from then on.

She woke early. Ciro was watching her in silence. It wasn't normal for him to wake up before her. Ruth smiled and he headed for the bathroom without returning the smile.

"Is everything okay?" she asked.

"Everything's fine," he replied.

For years on end, Ruth would go over that morning in her mind. She was sure Ciro still loved her when he went to bed, but he woke up changed, sullen, dry. He had come home late, he'd been drinking, and Ruth had wanted to talk, but he'd become irritated and locked himself in the bathroom. The next day, he was aloof. She demanded an explanation and heard something she'd never expected: the problem was their marriage. Ruth froze. He didn't want to get into it now, apologized, buttoned up his suit, and left for the office. Shaken, she asked the maid to look after João, called in sick to work, and retreated to the bedroom. The maid noticed her pale face, bulging eyes, and shortness of breath, but didn't say anything. She took care of the boy.

Ruth didn't eat, sleep, or leave her cloister. Midnight came and went and there was no sign of Ciro. She began to panic. She fell asleep exhausted, with swollen eyes, woke up in a sweat, and began to pace back and forth. She looked out the window every minute. She talked to herself and sobbed, while insomnia came and went. The sun was about to rise when she heard the door. Like a trained dog missing its owner, she stood waiting beside the bed. She heard footsteps in the corridor, it was him, she was sure. The door opened and Ciro appeared, unsettled.

Ruth ignored the lipstick marks and glitter on his shirt. They went at it like dogs. Ruth sobbed, clinging to her husband, and he swore he'd been faithful.

The months passed uneventfully, Ciro seemed cured, and Ruth recovered her delicate pride. The television was flooded with Christmas commercials, announcing the bottleneck of festivities. Ciro said he was going to stay back late for the firm's end-of-year shindig. Ruth didn't mind, overwhelmed as she was with presents, tree, and turkey, with the French toast and desserts for Christmas Eve. Midnight arrived and Ciro was nowhere to be seen. She went to bed with the sinking feeling that the nightmare was back. At 4:47 in the morning, she heard the key in the lock and raced into the corridor, tail wagging. Ciro had gone on a bender, as he did occasionally. His fly down, shirt hanging out of his pants, and traces of cheap cherry lipstick gave him away. Ciro showed no sign of guilt or regret; on the contrary, he laughed and called her darling. Disgusting. She shoved him away and shouted so that the neighbors would all know what a vile creature shared her bed with her. She gave full rein to hysteria. Ciro lost his patience. He'd been up all night and needed to sleep. He grabbed a change of clothes and disappeared through the back door. Her voice quieted when she saw him take the elevator down, and she spent the night standing in the laundry room, watching the back door. The maid arrived at seven and Ruth ran to lock herself in the bedroom. She took charge of the boy, the kitchen, and the ironing, and didn't call Ruth until late in the afternoon, to say she had to go. It was December 23. Ruth didn't answer. The poor woman called Raquel, the boy's aunt, to ask her to take over. Raquel sent João to stay with his cousins and tried to coax Ruth out of her refuge. It was a lengthy negotiation. Ruth said she would only leave the room if Ciro came to her. Raquel repeated that she would leave a message in the living room, in case he came back, but that she needed to keep her chin up and lean on her family.

"You need to think of João, Ruth. It's not his fault you two aren't seeing eye to eye. Think about it—João's more important than Ciro."

Ruth loved João, but she had Ciro on a pedestal. That was why she hadn't wanted any more children—she didn't need them. It was a character flaw, highly irrational, a curse. She came out of hiding after much insistence, pallid and almost dead. Raquel was shocked by her sister's withdrawal. She helped her into the car as if she were made of crystal and took her to her home in Humaitá. Ruth didn't come down for supper on Christmas Eve, nor did she want to open presents or see relatives. She stopped eating on the 29th and continued to fast until the 31st. She was admitted to Clínica São Vicente on January 1, 1981.

Ciro didn't show up until the afternoon, in a fluster, and begged to be alone with his wife. Raquel reluctantly agreed. She needed to rest, and she really did believe her brother-in-law had an obligation to clean up his mess. Ruth woke up hours later. When she saw Ciro, she thought the sedative was making her hallucinate. He lay down beside her and swore once more that he'd never do it again. Ruth took his word for it. She had no choice, and would have done anything so as not to lose him again. Ruth belonged to Ciro. And the more she proved it, the harder it was for Ciro to love what he had.

Six more months of calm and then another silly slip, a missed dentist appointment for João, made Ruth prick up her ears. And for good reason. Ciro was carrying on with the wife of a client for whom he had won a case. Fear made her forget her dignity. She followed him in a taxi to Glória, took the elevator up to Sílvio's lair, caught them in the act, and made a scene. Ciro acted as if there was no one else there, stood, dressed calmly, and disappeared down the corridor. Ruth screamed until she lost her voice, stumbled down the nine flights of stairs, went to the corner, wandered around in circles looking for him, came to her senses, felt ridiculous, and went home. Ciro was already there, showered and in pajamas. When he saw her, he smiled as if everything was normal. Bewildered, Ruth told him what had happened and Ciro acted indignant. He lamented the fiasco, was concerned about Sílvio, whose apartment it was, and assured her that she had disturbed the wrong couple. He had been there at home the whole time, waiting for her.

"Don't you think you should see a doctor, my love?"

Ruth lowered herself onto a chair using the back as a support. She asked for a glass of water. If it wasn't him, she thought, who had she seen in Glória? And if it was him in Glória, then who was the pajama-clad man standing before her in the dining room now? It consumed her to such an extent that once again she forgot to eat and sleep. She was admitted to the clinic again three days later.

Ruth came back changed. She barely spoke and was secretive. She understood that people thought she was crazy, but she didn't care. Her disappointment with Ciro extended to the rest of humanity. She didn't give a damn about anyone. We only love what we don't have. It had taken her years to heed the warning. She had done everything wrong, she had never resisted Ciro. She had given in immediately, for all time. She had lost all bargaining power. She needed to deprive him of her. Ruth stopped talking to her husband.

Ruth was wrong in thinking that she could make passion succumb to her will. The one who suffered was her. She was the one missing him. She was a masochist when Ciro wanted her to be a sadist. It destroyed their sex life. Ciro reacted with equal violence. He fucked half of Rio, while Ruth looked on in silence.

The most extreme act of romanticism is suicide. Ruth was born with the flaw of being exceedingly feminine and overly romantic. She had always seen it as an advantage, but now that she had discovered how fragile she was, she'd have given anything to be free of herself. If she had the audacity of Madame Bovary, she'd have taken hemlock; if she had the nobility of Sonya, she'd have taken on Siberia; if she were poor, like Fantine, she'd have pulled out her teeth. But no, she was a mortal, middle-class woman from Rio, like so many others. Célia, Irene, and Raquel all treated her suffering as something vulgar—it was just a separation. Wrist-slitting, hanging, gas, these were ends too grandiose for someone like her. She decided to be humble and kill her love with vestal discretion; her home became a convent. She no longer planned to win back her husband. What she wanted was to insulate herself from the noise outside; she didn't want to care, to want, to need, to suffer. Death. She practiced indifference until she became insensitive to the smell, face, and voice of her other half. Objects began to disappear from the apartment, records, books. Ciro was preparing to move out. He hung his head and left, his suitcases full. Ruth understood that he wouldn't be back. She was relieved, free to be unhappy on her own terms.

"Ruth, Ciro died, yesterday, at Silvestre. They found a really aggressive tumor three months ago. He didn't make it. It's over, Ruth," said Raquel. "Do you want to go to the funeral? I have to take João and I thought I should ask you."

Ruth was furious at her sister. Her repressed love threatened to well up and spill over. She would never see Ciro again. All that was left was her mistakes, she thought. Ciro would never know that their ten years of marriage continued to mean everything to her. Why hadn't Raquel told her before? She wanted to slap her, blame her for his murder. Her long training in isolation, the self-control attained at great cost, brought back her rationality. It was for the best, she thought. She wouldn't have had the courage to see him, to risk losing her sanity once again. She said she'd rather stay home.

Raquel left the room without protest. She had learned to respect her sister's sovereign will. She had adopted João as her own and had kept on the maid. Ruth required very little; in exchange she asked that no one judge her, and that she be left in peace. Raquel had grown up jealous of her sister's charms, but now she thanked God that such divine gifts had not been bestowed upon her. She had learned from a young age that the world is unfair and that great joys precede even greater tragedies. She despised her brother-in-law for his weakness and considered not attending the funeral herself, but her sense of duty toward her nephew made her forget the idea.

Ruth opened a cupboard in the living room that hadn't seen any light since Ciro had left. She took out a dusty cardboard box, placed it on the table, and rummaged through the pile of records looking for the old Dolores Duran LP. The record player, along with the sound system that Ciro had bought in 1978, was still intact in the cabinet. The maid tended to the empty rooms with the same zeal as before. Ruth was always in the bedroom, but that day, after Raquel knocked on her door, she decided to come out of hiding. She opened the curtains of the living room to let in the sun and allow her memory to roam. She saw herself, so different to the person she was now, sitting on that same sofa, Ciro inviting her to dance, João jumping on the cushions, the paintings, the table. The moment required music. She took the record out of its cover, cleaned it carefully, and put it on the turntable. The needle was still there, the crackling before the melody began, the orchestra's introduction, Dolores.

Don't let the bad world take you away again

Ruth turned up the volume, sang, danced, and allowed herself to be swept away. The she flopped onto the armchair, out of breath, pensive, and fell silent. She was grateful. She had lived with Ciro's absence for years. His death had put an end to the unbearable possibility of one day discovering that he was happy with another woman. Dead, he would remain hers, immaterial, eternal.

*   *   *

Ruth outlived everyone in her generation. She lasted for many years, locked away in her apartment with her imaginary partner. She checked out from reality early, existing somewhere between here and there, more there than here. Alzheimer's, abulia, dementia, sclerosis—so many names for such similar symptoms. Ruth extinguished herself, watched over by her sister, and passed away one rainy morning at the age of eighty-three, happy with her master.

CÉLIA WAS THERE for Ruth throughout her drama, kept her up to date on Ciro's latest, was present every time she was admitted to the clinic, until she came to the conclusion that her friend's neurosis was a lost cause.

After the divorce, Célia's visits to the ground-floor apartment on Rua Maria Angélica came to an end. The ample living room opening onto a well-kept garden, where in the past they'd met for Saturday feijoadas, watched the World Cup, where the children could run free and the adults could play cards and drink all they wanted, became a dark mausoleum. Ruth didn't open the windows or turn on the light. She inhabited the last bedroom, and no one was allowed in except the maid. But she didn't consider the maid a person, Célia suspected, judging by the way Ruth addressed her.

"I'm telling you, Irene, Ruth acts like a plantation owner. She treats the maid like a slave and has breakfast in bed. If she'd only fold some clothes or wash some dishes, she wouldn't be like this, desperate because of that good-for-nothing husband of hers. I know I'm a bother, so I won't be going back. What for? To listen to her majesty's tantrums?"

Irene didn't disagree, although she thought Célia was exaggerating somewhat. She identified more with Ruth than

154

with Célia, the Margaret Thatcher of São Cristóvão. Irene avoided talking about her own marital dissatisfaction with Célia for fear she'd get a lecture.

Célia had studied at a public school, was a swimming champion in junior high, and knew how to stand up for herself. Her Portuguese father had been abandoned by his mother, who had become widowed early and, preferring the company of her oldest son, had sent the younger one to boarding school. Her rejection gave the boy a trade. He learned carpentry at school and, once he was fully grown and the master of his own destiny, did well for himself in furniture-making. He married his shop's cleaner, a beautiful black woman with very white teeth, who turned out to be a splendid business manager. Célia grew up near the São Cristóvão Club soccer field. She liked to go to Quinta da Boa Vista Park after Sunday mass, to games at Maracanã Stadium, and for ice cream and a movie at Saenz Peña Square. Rio's North Zone was her territory. But prosperity and the purchase of a large shop in Catete made the family move to Flamengo when she was eighteen. This social ascension was terrible for Célia. She didn't recognize herself in that amoral paradise—she was from the working class. When she finished technical school, she didn't even consider going to university, as she despised academic pride. They like to rub those scrolls in our faces, she used to say. Célia wanted a job, a wage, and independence. She took a typing course and was hired as a trainee with the state traffic department. She prospered in that bureaucratic cesspool, surrounded by underhanded schemes, the buying of driver's licenses, kickbacks, expediters, dust, and no air conditioning. She treated the rich and the poor with equal steeliness. She did justice. She didn't turn in her colleagues, and hated snitches, but she refused to take part in their thievery. Deep down, they're all no good, she thought.

She had never trusted men; she'd been brought up not to. Tall and athletic, the only reason she didn't have more suitors was because young men were intimidated by that Charles de Gaulle in a skirt. The opposite sex was a potential enemy and she looked down on them from the heights of her fortress. Only a saint could get to her. The saint, in this case, was Neto.

Célia swam from one end of Copacabana to the other on a regular basis. From the sand near Fort Copacabana, Neto saw Calypso emerge from the waves. Of mixed ancestry, like himself, a giant, extraordinary. He fell for her there and then.

Lover boy had a degree in business management. His father, a public servant, had brought his son up to be someone. He drank in moderation and was a good kid, good-humored, and brilliant at soccer. Álvaro attributed Neto's excessive normality to his skin color. His theory wasn't unfounded. Whenever a more raucous celebration ended with the police at the door, Neto was always the one hauled down to the station. This unspoken racism made him pursue an exemplary life. He married young, had children young, and died young.

He had met Ciro and Álvaro at university. Business Management had a few subjects in common with Law and Accounting. Together, they'd started a samba-jazz band, with Neto on drums and Ciro on the guitar. Álvaro had tried the tambourine, but had ended up on the shaker.

They were united by male allegiance, women, and the beach, in that order. Copacabana was home to various tribes. Álvaro had known Ribeiro since he was a child. They had both lived on Ministro Rocha Azevedo and had gone to the beach at the end of Rua Miguel Lemos. Ribeiro was friends with the crowd there, some rough types who ran amok in the nice neighborhood. He was always surrounded by women, unlike Álvaro, who frightened them away even when he still had hair. Sílvio was drawn to the group by Ciro's charms, and took everyone's virginity in psychoactives. Sílvio was a myth in Copacabana. He was said to be the youngest person ever accepted into the famous Jackass Club, and had participated in the cowardly act of hanging a transvestite by the foot from a tenth-floor window on Rua Barata Ribeiro.

The first Carnival of the 1960s was the big turning point in their friendship. Sílvio told them about some Italians he'd met in the diplomatic service, who pretended to be gay to get close to virgins and women who were hard to get. "They loosen up because they think they're safe . . . after two drinks you're in!" he assured them. He proposed they use their musical talents to found their own Carnival block of cross-dressing men. The idea was greeted with unconditional enthusiasm.

They spent the entire month of February putting together their costumes. Ciro, the most beautiful of them all, played a sexy intellectual and launched the miniskirt way before Mary Quant, with boots and a wig with a fringe. Álvaro was a housewife with watermelon breasts, and Neto let out his inner samba queen in a dazzling gold-sequined bikini, with a boa around his shoulders and feathers on his head. Sílvio went as Carmen Miranda, and Ribeiro paid tribute to Norma Bengell's Bardot. They laid half the city and consolidated their friendship.

Neto's friends were his only sin.

The five were lolling in the sand when the goddess emerged from the waves and strode to the shade of the beach tent next to theirs. The skin on muscle, the sway of her hips, and her hard thighs were an arrow through Neto's heart. His friends noticed and began to egg him on. Neto approached her. Célia was aloof and kept him on ice for months. She didn't give him the time of day, but she didn't discourage him either. His extreme patience was proof of his love. Then she tortured him with a year of courting and a three-year engagement. A virgin. The bride's parents only gave their consent to the marriage after the groom was given a promotion at the hospital supply company he worked for. Neto bravely resisted the urge to swallow Célia alive, to be alone with her, without her mother, nieces, cousins, aunts, and uncles. Without clothes. He could barely wait. At the wedding ceremony he was so anxious, so thankful to finally have the right to be with his own wife, that he sobbed at the altar. The long wait annulled his performance that first night. His blood pressure dropped and he had to lie down. Exhausted from all the anticipation, he fell asleep. Célia didn't mind leaving consummation until the next morning. She hugged her trophy husband and took a while to nod off. You only became a grown-up when you were married, and now she was. Married and a grown-up.

Her father had a meltdown at the church. He started muttering inaudibly in the sacristy. Then he began to roll his head around, gesticulating and flinging his arms wide.

"That bastard . . . that bastard's going to steal my daughter . . . "

Family members tried to reassure him, but he lost his composure, repeating that they were taking his baby girl. The mother, worried that his deep-seated jealousy would ruin the occasion, gave him a tranquilizer, told him to splash some water on his face, and went back to enjoy her day of glory. She had been born in the neighborhood of Mangueira, had lost her parents at a young age, and had helped bring up her brothers and sisters. She had never imagined that she would be able to give her daughter a wedding like that. She had a photograph of the bride and groom framed and hung it in the living room over the couch. Poverty, the death of her parents and many other relatives, it was all behind her now. All she had to do was sit and wait for grandchildren.

They took a while to come. A boy and a girl, Murilo and Dalva. Célia put together a spreadsheet of their expenses and calculated that it would be wise to wait three years before having a child. Every month, she would set aside part of their earnings for the future endeavor and, in the meantime, enjoyed her prince consort.

They were happy together.

Célia put up with Neto's friends' mischief until their children were born. Then she removed them all from her circle of trust. She was suspicious of Sílvio's fetishes and Ribeiro's pedophilia. Her father died begging her not to let down her guard. "Sons-in-law aren't relatives," he insisted. Her mother argued with him, defending her daughter's choice, but thought it didn't hurt to stay alert.

Serial divorces, youths on drugs, hippies in dirty pants: Célia hated the new ways of the world. She never forgot the day she saw Ney Matogrosso on television for the first time. At first she admired the folk singer with the beautiful voice, with a splendid feather boa around her shoulders and a vulture mask on her face. Célia thought she was a little hairy, but the pitch of her voice was unmistakable: it was a woman. In a more daring dance move, the mysterious peacock thrust its hips this way, while the breast baubles went that way, revealing that there were no breasts there.

"It's a man!" she cried. "Good Lord! It's a man!"

Célia made the children leave the room.

"The world's gone crazy," she said to Neto that evening, and redoubled her watch over her children.

She admired President Médici and General Geisel, and shared their horror of communists. They wanted to take over Brazil, she was sure of it. What, share my home with others? Let them do it at their own place! And she would turn her back, refusing to give it any more thought. Her two biggest fears were that Dalva would lose her virginity and that Murilo would be gay. Her paranoia about external threats ended up molding her appearance. She became dour. The tension around her mouth creased her cheeks, and worry etched out lines in her forehead and grooves between her eyebrows. Célia grew ugly. Neto didn't notice. To him, she would always be Calypso.

They fought, it is true, many times, and even came to blows once or twice, but breaking up was never a possibility. Célia was the guard dog of the family. She died without enjoying an old age, at sixty, of a stroke. It would have been an exemplary death if she hadn't been so young. She said goodnight to her husband, went to bed, and didn't wake up.

Neto's desperation at his wife's wake was a sign of what was to come. He doubled over in anguish. He knelt on the ground, tried to tear off his clothes, gnashed his teeth, kicked, and shouted. His children ran to restrain him. Neto's howling diminished, his fury abated, and Murilo and Dalva sat him down once again in the chairs beside their mother, but the calm didn't last. The queue of condolence-givers had barely begun to move again when Neto had another wild fit. He seized Célia and tried to carry her out of there, to take her home. Help was needed to get him to put her body down. At Murilo's request, Álvaro and Ribeiro dragged him off to the infirmary. Sedated, he followed the coffin, leaning on two of the sidekicks his wife had so vehemently disliked.

Neto never recovered. Of his own accord, he continued taking the tranquilizers he'd been given at São João Batista Cemetery. "I can't take this sober," he said. When his speech became so slurred that no one could understand what he was saying, Murilo took him to a psychiatrist and Neto began the merry-go-round of trial and error with mood regulators. None worked very well. The cocktail turned him into a walking bundle of side effects. He would swing from euphoria to depression, more depressed than euphoric. Murilo tried homeopathy, massage, acupuncture, and insisted on psychoanalysis, but nothing could put a dent in Neto's fixation with Célia.

He was in permanent mourning.

NETO

*December 27, 1929
†April 30, 1992

CÉLIA WATCHED the evening news and went to lie down. "It's early," I argued, but she wasn't feeling well. I watched a war movie and went to bed too. The next day I was surprised to find her still in bed when I woke up. Célia usually rose before me to fix breakfast. I showered and dressed, but she didn't move. When I tried to wake her, I realized that she was stiff. Célia had died in the middle of the night, beside me; an aneurysm took her without me noticing. That very instant, all the bad times disappeared: her moods, her aversion to my friends, her nagging our daughter-in-law, her surliness toward our son-in-law, her chronic unhappiness, the disagreements, the slaps. I was washed over with unconditional love for the two of us, for our years together. I was paralyzed, sitting on the bed, reminiscing, without the courage to be practical.

My son arranged everything: funeral home, mass, chapel. He chose a beautiful coffin. I was unfit for anything. I sat beside her at the wake, and people came to talk to me, but I wasn't there, I wasn't anywhere. I wanted to step out of my own skin, step out of me. I roared, shouted, blasphemed, but it didn't help—I haven't come down to this day. Sober, never again. I refuse to start all over; I've lost the illusion you need to be able to reinvent the days.

I had to be carried at the funeral. Álvaro and Ribeiro propped me up. A bell rang to announce that the coffin was leaving and we dragged ourselves through the cemetery. Good God, it's sad. Afterward, I hugged my children and grandchildren and came home to the apartment I'd lived in with Célia for over thirty years. The silence was piercing, I ran to turn on the TV. Murilo thought he'd better sleep with me that first night. It was as weird for him as it was for me. The next day I sent him home. I had to learn to be on my own, I told him while looking him in the eye, pretending to have come to my senses.

I've been trying for a year, but it all seems artificial: going out, catching a movie, having dinner. I have no one to talk to about the news anymore, it's as if there were no more facts. The sun rises and sets in a sequence of hours that are all the same. Célia was the connection, our home existed thanks to her. She was paranoid, mistrustful, and critical of Ciro, Sílvio, Álvaro, and Ribeiro from the day she met them. What does it matter? I didn't know it until I saw her body lying there on the bed—I didn't know it but Célia was my pillar, my mast, my rock.

I close the windows, check to see if I've left the door open, the fridge, the gas—I'm methodical. I turn off the lights and lock myself in the bedroom. I try to read, I can't. I've always liked reading, but I can't anymore. I've become impervious to other people's dramas.

How can anyone go on without plans? At the age of twenty, people assassinate loves, friendships, they move on like a sharp arrow; it is only later that they discover how rare real affection is. I don't believe in passion late in life; people don't love after forty. It's a lie. At the most, they make a formal pact, pretend to miss and to appreciate one another, but biology doesn't need the juvenile outbursts of an old man.

My friends never understood my connection with Célia. And she didn't exactly help matters. She hated them all, especially Sílvio. The day Suzana smoked pot in Ciro's garden, she started in the minute we got home, saying we needed to talk. She said she didn't want her son to be around that pack, she was afraid Sílvio might abuse Murilo, she'd heard of millions of cases of molestation by people close to the family. She brought up Irene's effeminate nephew, initiated by an uncle in the garage—that poor mother. I flew off the handle, saying that Murilo wasn't even a year old and that no pedophile disguised as a friend was going to attack our baby, much less Álvaro, Ciro, Sílvio, or Ribeiro, because they liked me. Ciro wanted to celebrate the fact that I'd become a father, and you had to feel sorry for Ribeiro, always chasing after younger women.

"Everyone smokes dope these days, Célia, and the one thing you can't do is stop me teaching Murilo to be a man. He really might become a fag if his mother points out a deviant on every corner. I'm not going to keep my son away from my friends because of a first-time mother's paranoia."

She put her head down, offended. Murilo started to cry and Célia, her eyes full of tears, said it was time to nurse him. We never touched on the subject again.

That was our routine: quibbles, arguments, hurt feelings, and making up. I became addicted to it, I didn't know how to live without it. Disagreeing with Célia kept me going. And we knew how to sweep it all under the rug, which is fundamental to the health of any relationship. You have to turn the page, forget, wipe the slate clean, forgive, let go of things. Women refuse to understand and insist on trotting out their stupid reasons. They want to change their men, make them into princes. Men just watch, hoping they'll get tired of it, and go on repeating the same old mistakes. Women scold, curse, shout, cry, and then they go fix dinner. Even feminists go fix dinner. And we stay together until one of us goes and leaves the other one here, in the grave.

I'm sitting on the armchair in the living room. I was about to go to bed, but then I did an about-face and ended up here. The apartment is the same, I haven't rearranged the furniture or given her clothes away. But I feel different. I woke up different today: a morbid peace came over me, a distance I'd never felt before. That was when I heard her voice. It happened to me once before, in the foyer, but never again. Today it's back. It's more like a breath, a gust, a whiff of her. It was in the morning, when I went to the chest of drawers to get some money for the bakery. That's why I'm sitting here, thinking about it, about the breeze that ran through me.

Célia was white, or considered white, because she had delicate features, but she was half-black, like me, and used to straighten her hair, which was kinky, like mine. My four best friends were white. They didn't know the pressure of being a different color, of not looking like any of your peers or the people in your building, your neighborhood, of looking more like the cleaners, street sweepers, and construction workers who serve white people like themselves. When the sexual revolution arrived in Rio de Janeiro, Ciro, Sílvio, and Ribeiro—and even Álvaro, because of Irene, who'd started analysis—all became lost in that rampant debauchery. Babylon. Divorce became an obligation. I saw the scorn with which they looked at me, as they tossed away their marriages, one after another, in a rash of unchecked greed. It was suicidal, solitary, sterile. But not me. Frivolity isn't me. I got the best grades, passed the worst tests, boiled my brains studying, worked like a dog, and never cheated. I was honest to a fault.

Enough.

I want to write a note. Where's the pen? On the shelf. And the paper? In the drawer. Nothing out of place. Except me. I'm going to sit down and write. What was it I wanted to write? A note. I take the lid off the Bic, place it beside the blank page, rest the tip of the ballpoint pen on the smooth surface, and write, "Don't tell anyone." Why did I write that? It's for my kids, I think. I fold the paper and put it in my pocket. Now I can go to bed. I walk down the long corridor of closed doors. I don't like this narrow funnel—it reminds me of the mess, the towels on the ground, the panties hanging from the faucet, and the lack of them, the lack of her. I turn right into the bathroom next to the bedroom. When we moved into this apartment, there was no talk of en suites, balconies, play areas, or covered parking. The rooms were large and that was enough. We lived with each other's smells, vapors, strands of hair, and puddles.

Her toothbrush looks at me from the cup by the sink. It's still there. I open the cupboard behind the mirror and stop with the door half-open. The mirror is the same as the day we set foot in here for the first time. It's cracked. I look for my old face, it's me, there, and it's not; I don't remember what I looked like anyway. I open it. Ritalin, Lexapro, Frontal, Valium, Haldol, Seroquel, the rest of the Pondera from last year, and the Aropax that Dr. Péricles plans to try on me in the next few months. The labels stare at me from the hole in the wall. Murilo insisted that I get help. For a whole year I answered endless questions about the effects of the benzodiazepines on my system. Dr. Péricles wanted to know about my urges, anxiety, low spirits in the morning, and then, according to my answers, he would change the dosage, which would lead to new sets of questions. "This one works better, that one worse," I would answer, like a well-behaved pupil, until I suddenly became an uncooperative guinea pig. I decided not to collaborate with the labs anymore and avenged myself systematically, messing with their precious research. I gave them fraudulent data and complained of dizziness, chest pains that didn't exist. I proved to be a dangerous, anarchical rat, out to undermine the scientific megalomania of mood regulators, frustrate those who thought they could control my misery. I felt considerably better during that period— I enjoyed seeing the doctor's surprise at the symptoms I described. It was obvious that Péricles was lost. He was lost even before I started faking symptoms. A medical doctor would be able to diagnose fake pancreatitis, but the psych Péricles went strictly by American statistics, the behavioral tables put out by Pfizer, by Roche, without realizing that I was doing what man has done from day one: lying and having fun. There is no remedy for that. I actually felt a little sorry for him. I was grateful to Péricles. He was the one who talked Murilo out of having me go through psychoanalysis. I went to a few sessions but I didn't make it past the first month. The analyst was a bore who charged a fortune to sit there with his mouth shut, me with my back to him, giving voice to my neuroses. A pathetic scene. Who invented that crap? Old regrets should be left well alone. Célia and I are the best example of that.

Pulling the rug on Péricles' certainties lost its appeal recently, two appointments ago. He handed me the prescription, I stopped by the pharmacy and brought home the collection of little bottles. I put them in the bathroom cupboard with the cracked mirror without even opening them. I stopped taking them. For the last three weeks my moods have been free to roam. And now they've taken over.

I take the bottles with the black-label warnings and put them in my pocket, then I fill a glass with water straight from the faucet. Why filter? I glance at the darkened living room, then turn on the light in the corridor and head for the bedroom. I lock the door purely out of habit, as no one is going to come barging in, sit on the bed, and deposit the bottles and glass on the bedside table. I take off my blazer, shirt, and pants and hang them on the hat rack. I sit down again.

"The difference between black-label and red-label warnings," the pharmacy assistant told me, "is that if you take the whole bottle of black ones you croak; not so with the red ones." He said it and laughed, placing the three bottles in the basket. What's so funny? I thought.

"Yes, what's so funny?"

The air becomes heavy all of a sudden. I realize I'm not alone. There is someone besides me, there, on the bed. I can hear them breathing. I don't dare turn to see who it is. I slide my fingers over the sheet, fumbling in the dark, until a familiar hand grasps mine.

"Aren't you coming to bed?"

The voice echoes clearly in the empty room. I take a moment to answer, fearing the illusion will unravel.

"I'm coming."

"What time is it?"

"Late," I say.

"Aren't you coming to bed?"

I close my eyes and lean over slowly, holding her hand so that it can't leave mine. Staring at the ceiling, without the courage to move, I feel the volume of a body snuggle up to mine. Hers.

"I thought it was morning already," she says.

"No, it's still dark out, you were in a deep sleep."

We lie there quietly in each other's arms.

"Is something wrong?"

"I can't sleep."

"Is it work?"

"No, Célia, it has nothing to do with work. It's me."

I close my eyes tighter and push her away from me. I touch her hair, her chest, her waist, belly, hips, I wish so badly for it to be real. I move my eyelids gingerly, light invades my retinas and shows me Célia's face. She is neutral. She isn't young, but she doesn't have the lines of her later testiness either. She is a beautiful woman. My woman. My wife.

"What's wrong?" she asks, with a slight smile. "Nothing," I reply.

I always envied Ciro's love for Ruth. He came to the beach the day after Juliano's party and invited me to go for a swim. He was more handsome than ever. We passed the wave-break and Ciro confessed that he was in love with the singer from the night before. Ruth was her name. They had spent the night together and Cupid had pierced him with his arrow.

"I didn't think this existed, Neto, you know what I mean?"

"No, I don't."

"Love is much more violent than I thought. Fucking someone with this intensity, screwing a woman who belongs to you, who's yours by destiny, by birthright, past lives, who knows. I didn't expect it to happen to me, I thought it was all bullshit. Now I can't live without her, Neto. I want to marry her, have kids with her, fuck, die, kill for her."

I felt sorry for myself. The waves rose up behind us and he caught the next one, the biggest, body-surfing it all the way to the sand, letting out a Tarzan cry.

There really was an aura around them. It wasn't like that with Célia and me. I loved her, but it wasn't like that. Ruth and Ciro extinguished themselves in a fire. They were joined at the hip, at the shoulder; but even though Ciro was head over heels in love with Ruth, he kept looking for that poetic, romantic flame, that yearning that he revealed to me on the beach at the beginning of their life together. Ciro would fight with her and come back, just to create the expectation that Ruth might leave him. He knew she was incapable of it. But he needed her to, so he could win her over again, fuck her as if for the first time. Ruth never got it. She suffered, a slave to his eroticism. Passion is a serious illness. Ciro needed her to be stronger than him, but she wasted away like the most ordinary of women. He became so desperate that he tried to seduce the door, the skirting board. The tragedy was that he never found another Ruth, the Ruth from the early days, the one who still didn't belong to him, even though she did. The staidness of my marriage was always frustrating, but now, looking at Célia lying beside me, I am gripped by Ciro and Ruth's ardor. The commotion of belonging to someone. This discovery didn't come in a flash, in the dawn of my life—I have only just become aware of it, after her death. Here, in our mahogany bed, I understand what Ciro wanted to tell me that afternoon, when we passed the wave-break.

"Aren't you going to sleep?" she insists.

"I don't know."

"Why don't you take something to help you?"

I am silent, considering the possibility.

"Do you dream, Célia?"

"No."

"Don't you miss dreaming?"

"No."

"What about you, do you dream?"

"Sometimes, about you."

"Take something, it'll do you good. Want me to get it for you?" she asks.

"Yes, please," I say.

Célia gets up, as she always used to, the day dawning outside, puts on her slippers, walks around the bed, chooses one of the bottles on the bedside table and sits beside me.

"How many are you supposed to take?"

"I don't know, how many do you think I should take? Did you read the instructions?"

She unfolds the paper and puts on my glasses to read the fine print.

"Who prescribed this?"

"Dr. Péricles, the psychiatrist."

"Did you read the side effects?"

"I did . . . Scary."

"Constipation, sweating, panic attacks, allergic reactions, liver damage . . . Who referred you to this guy?"

"Murilo."

"Oh . . . how is he?"

"He's well. We brought up one fine kid. Two—him and Dalva."

She gives a satisfied smile.

"How many do you want to take?"

"I don't know, I just want to sleep."

"A whole bottle?"

"I guess so, if it doesn't do the job I can take another one. There's water in the glass."

"Best leave the note where it can be seen," she suggests.

"It's in my blazer."

She goes over to the hat rack, takes the piece of folded paper out of my pocket, and doesn't know where to put it.

"You think it's a bad idea to leave it in my pocket?"

"I'm afraid they might not see it."

"What about on the bedside table?"

"Move the glass so the paper doesn't get wet."

She tips half the content of the bottle into the palm of my hand and waits with the lid open. I swallow the first round of pills.

"Just one more and you're done."

She gives me the rest and I wash them down with the last of the water, then I lie down to wait. Célia pulls the covers up to my neck, kisses me, and returns to her side of the bed. I just lie there looking at the ceiling.

A sleepy drunkenness comes over me and I doze, wake, and snooze again. I don't know how long I spend coming and going like this. Suddenly, a sharp pain in my stomach jolts me out of my trance. My stomach heaves, my intestines tighten, my heart speeds up, a twinge announces the horror to come. Cold sweat, cramps, uncontrollable vomiting. I stand quickly and drag myself to the toilet. I throw up on all fours and sit down on the cold floor to breathe. There's more to come. Or isn't there? I lean on the wall to stand, rinse my mouth out with toothpaste, and try to go back to the bedroom. I stop short in the doorway. My stomach heaves again and I drop to the floor. And again, and again. Bile. Nothing left to come out. I straighten up, breathe, settle. I go into the bedroom. The bed is empty. She should be here. She isn't anymore. I call her name, there is no answer. I search under the sheets, open and close the doors of the built-in wardrobe, look under the bed. She's gone. I forget the nausea, heartburn, and pain, and head down the corridor. I fling open the doors of Murilo's and Dalva's bedrooms, the study, I go into the kitchen, to the laundry room, I turn the living room upside down—no sign of her. I collapse in the armchair.

Meanwhile, an insidious rancor, an aggressive impulse, small but concrete enough to be felt, grows in me until it reaches my head. I hate her for leaving me here on my own without finishing what she came here to do.

Go ahead and vanish, you sadistic bitch, disappear. Thirty years of quarreling and, now, the last dagger. I loved you a lot, Célia. After you disappeared I loved you like I never thought I'd love anyone. I thought you'd understood it there, in the bed, in the way I gazed at you, hugged you, and celebrated your presence. Is this revenge? Is that it? Thirty years of putting up with your scowl only to have you disappear again? Nice one, Célia, nice one.

You didn't even give me the pleasure of leaving you. Not even that. The morning I arrived home in a daze after Sílvio's farewell, there, that day, I should have left you. I never told you what happened in the twelve hours leading up to that morning, nor did you want to know. I forgot about you that night, Célia, I swallowed everything that Sílvio gave me, I drank all I could, danced, sang, and hugged my badly-behaved friends; I was theirs, just theirs. I dragged a blond into the guest toilet and when she unzipped my fly, she was shocked at what she found. You should have seen how happy she was, how appreciative. You never mentioned it, not even in our fantasies, you never praised me the way she did. I'm not just any old guy, Célia, you know that. How can you not be grateful? Go ask Irene what it's like being married to someone who can't get it up. You pretended it wasn't important your whole life. You pretended so much that I ended up forgetting. But at that fancy party in Leme, which

Sílvio chose to say goodbye to us, with the blond kneeling in front of me, devout, incredulous, her mouth on my crotch, I remembered what I had between my legs. I tore off my clothes and headed for the dance floor. I wanted to show the world. I was removed forcefully. Outside, I was still raring to go and even took the last pill that Sílvio gave me. But when they all agreed to take the party to Glória, I realized I'd never be one of them. I was ashamed of what I'd done. I wanted to come home, sleep, switch off. The rest of my life—you, the kids, home, the office, the contracts—was all incompatible with the gutter, the whores, and the four pals I liked so much. I didn't have their courage. I came home, Célia, and you hit me with a closed fist, you hit me in the face, on my back. I took it. I should have disappeared forever, but I only went as far as the elevator. I needed to sleep. And I didn't come home because I loved you, Célia, I came back because I couldn't be like my friends. No matter how badly I wanted to, or tried, I'd never be one of them.

I spent the last year thinking I was suffering from lovesickness, but it was anger. I don't forgive you for being mean. I was an extraordinary, patient husband, a good father. What else did you want? The name for your acidity is vanity, Célia. I'm better than you. More humane, without a doubt. I'd have left you in peace; I wouldn't have spent a year prowling around your head, needling you, I wouldn't have come back here to commit euthanasia. Go fuck yourself, Célia. Take your things, disappear, and don't come back.

I attack the wardrobe, grab her clothes, hurl them out the window, return to the bathroom, throw her toothbrush into the toilet, and try to flush it down. I rummage through her things, tear up photos, kick boxes, hurl her shoes across the room. Another pang, the memory of the pain makes me double over. I regurgitate pills. I vomit in the maid's room. I drag myself to the bed and relax my head on the pillow. I'm not leaving here.

Wrath, finally, wrath. In recent months I'd forgotten how much I detested Célia. What a shame—now I want to carry on without her. It won't be possible. It would have been good. What a stupid thing I've done. My extremities grow numb, nothing moves, I have no more reflexes. All that is left is my thinking head, my bleary eyes, and my dry, bitter mouth.

Alone at last.

PADRE GRAÇA rose before dawn. He prayed, bathed, ate only a little, as he'd been trained to do, and arranged his liturgical objects in his small valise. São João Batista Cemetery awaited him.

He had recently assumed the position of chaplain at Rio de Janeiro's most traditional cemetery. It was a sin, he knew, but he couldn't contain his pride. With all due respect to John the Baptist, he identified more with Peter, gatekeeper of the eternal home. Padre Graça opened the earthly gates so that the saint could finish the job in heaven. Before getting to work, he liked to stroll through the lanes, admiring the ornate tombs and plaques paying homage to the dead. Occasionally he would change the dead flowers. On his way back to the chapel, after praying at the Sisters of São Vicente de Paulo quarter, he would visit Carmen Miranda, Villa-Lobos, and Luís Carlos Prestes. He was moved to come across Bento Ribeiro and Ary Barroso. It was paradise.

At the front office, he was informed that there were practically no services that day. In the morning, a middle-aged man, victim of a malignant tumor, and in the afternoon, an older gentleman. He donned his liturgical garments and climbed the stairs. Carpe diem. He wanted to take advantage of the fact that it wasn't a busy day and go all out on the prayer. In the corridor, he passed the funeral home staff—the deceased had just been sent to Chapel Ten. Padre Graça peered through a crack in the door. He didn't want to interrupt at the wrong moment. Three men were decorating the room. The tallest was arranging the lacy frills around the bier, while the bald one and the tanned one were discussing the best place to put the two wreaths behind the coffin. One had the short inscription: "In loving memory, from João," while the other read: "Friends forever, Álvaro, Neto, and Ribeiro." It was from the three men. Satisfied with the arrangement, they gazed at the gloomy composition. They were suffering.

Thinking this was the right moment, Padre Graça introduced himself and asked for details about Ciro. The ceremony required a summary of the deceased's life, and the priest wanted to prepare something special for the occasion. They gave him the basics: place of birth, age, marital status, profession, the name of his son, João, and cause of death. "He didn't even last six months," said Neto, unable to contain his emotion. They couldn't go on. Padre Graça tried to get additional information out of them, he formulated phrases, gave suggestions. "A good friend?" They agreed that yes, Ciro had been a good friend. "A good father?" Yes, they assured him he'd been a good father. But no description really did him justice.

—

Ciro was lust, beauty, irrationality. He was virginal love, adolescence, a man par excellence. The inventory of "good this and good that" wouldn't stop them from pining for the drinking binges, the wild nights, the attraction to the women he'd had. Ciro, Mr. Priest, was the quintessential Latin lover, the boxing champion, the Orpheus of Carnival, the faun, Cupid in person. Ciro was a god to the three of them. A fucking good-looking god, and flawed, because he was mortal. With nothing further to add, they hung their heads and consoled one another.

"Would any of you like to participate in the service?" Graça asked the laconic members of the flock.

Their refusal was unanimous. They reacted as one and fell silent at the same time, as if guided by telepathy.

"If Sílvio were here . . . " murmured Álvaro timidly.

Padre Graça had the impression they were laughing. They were. If the ambassador were here, they thought, lacking the courage to confess it to the priest, he'd be the one to deliver the eulogy. With his habitual calm and the aristocratic flair he'd acquired in the diplomatic service, Sílvio would challenge the prevailing moral code, shock relatives, and make Ciro's infinite lovers, who really did attend the funeral, blush. He would point out Ruth's absence, and tell the story of the couple's love and damnation. He would condemn monogamy. He would cite, one by one, the warrior's conquests and confess his own carnal attraction to his friend. Addressing Álvaro, Neto, and Ribeiro, he would decree the end of that group and finish by proposing an orgy in Glória, in memory of their late friend. Then they remembered, with sorrow, that they couldn't count on Sílvio's eloquence. By now, if they knew him at all, their balding blond pal, escorted by those mercenaries from the south, would be halfway to Bolivia on horseback, chewing coca leaves and practicing the Kama Sutra with the cholas of the Incan Empire.

"If you change your mind," insisted the priest, "come see me so we can discuss the timing."

And he left, focused on his notes, rehearsing the sermon in a low voice. Padre Graça was convinced that half a dozen phrases picked at random could relieve mourners' hearts. But from the difficulty he'd had with the trio, he gathered that "outstanding father," "exemplary husband," and "faithful companion" didn't exactly fit Ciro. He decided to focus on his premature death. He thought it would be a good idea to talk about acceptance and coming to terms with what seemed unjust.

*   *   *

"Let us meditate on eternity, and may we continue to realize that which God has placed in our hands. Let us do what is good and right."

When he finished quoting the passage, he was bursting with faith. He was a believer. Still a novice, he had assisted in one of the masses celebrated by the Saintly Pope, during

John Paul II's visit to Brazil. He had confirmed, there, his calling. Ten years later, Padre Graça was at the height of his Catholic enthusiasm, to the point of having visions like those of Saint Thérèse when he locked himself, alone, at night, in the cloister of a monastery in downtown Rio. In his ecstasy, he didn't notice that his listeners weren't paying attention. With the exception of Célia and one or two other elderly women, the dead man was surrounded by a front of practicing atheists. People who, in the desperation of the here and now, had lost all notion of what was good, honest, and upright.

Álvaro was gloating at seeing Irene left high and dry, dropped by the rowing club heartthrob. Neto and his wife weren't speaking by the time they arrived. She had made a snide remark about Ciro just before they left, and Neto had reacted by slapping her across the face. Ribeiro cursed the deceased for Ruth's ruin. João preferred to sit at a distance from his father's body, and Raquel, if she could have, would have spat in her ex-brother-in-law's face for allowing her nephew to take a back seat to the egotistical love that he and her crazy sister had shared. No one was thinking of Jesus, much less eternity. Cinira, the chubby girl from the office, was mourning the end of coffee-break escapades with her boss. Lílian was burying the pain of being dumped by Ciro on the Sunday of the roast chicken, and Milena was hobbling with the help of a cane, a result of the bullets her ex had put through her.

An admirable collection of adulteresses decked out the session with cleavage, silk stockings, and stilettos: a parade of coy gazes from Martas, Clarices and Gogoyas, plagued by sinful memories. God wasn't present, but Padre Graça didn't notice.

Without Ruth there, Álvaro, Neto, and Ribeiro accepted the condolences of those who knew Ciro from volleyball, from university, from the beach, colleagues from the office, old clients, and the succession of heartbroken women that never ceased to stream through the door. Middle-aged funerals are always the busiest.

With so many widows present, death slipped in unnoticed. When the priest asked for a moment of silence so that everyone might reflect on what was right, a fair-skinned brunette, not very tall, pushed her way through the crowd and only stopped when she leaned over the casket. Ciro. Álvaro, Neto, and Ribeiro followed the apparition with their eyes. We don't know that one, they thought. She was wearing a tight-waisted dress of shiny black velvet that showed off her generous hips. She gazed upon the dead man with an indecent, superior, consummated love. It was an irresistible sight. For the last time, they felt envious of their Don Juan.

She could barely recognize her victim's face in the light of the chapel, far from the hospital room and the tubes in his veins. He was better-looking like this than in bed, she thought. She had a thing for men in suits. Ciro's body was no exception. The trio continued to watch her attentively. The woman noticed the large turnout of female mourners and stopped to size them up. None of them had been as important as her. She was the widow there. She continued scrutinizing the room until she noticed Álvaro, Neto, and Ribeiro staring at her from the other side of the coffin. Padre Graça threw himself into the Lord's Prayer, but none of them were paying attention. Death admired the trio's elegance, their careful tie knots. Were they brothers? No, they were too different to have come from the same womb. She wanted to go to bed with all three of them. And then kill them, when the time was ripe. What else should she do? She had woken up like that, feeling generous. If she could choose, she'd take care of Neto first, then the others. She imagined him lying in bed, with her administering the sacrament. The mysterious figure's perverse gaze made Neto blush, and his two pals noticed. Célia noticed too. She hadn't taken her eyes off her husband, convinced that the five shared their furtive affairs. The insinuation had cost her the slap across the face, but now the slutty little widow justified Célia's desire to get him far away from there. She strode over to her husband, hooked her arm through his, and shot the rival a dirty look. The goddess scoffed at the shrew's vulgar jealously. She prayed that Célia would expire before everyone else present. Coincidence or not,

Neto would lose his wife the following year, and would die a year later himself.

"Amen," said the priest, and signaled for the procession to start.

Álvaro, Neto, and Ribeiro shared the coffin handles with Ciro's colleagues from work. The lover no one knew made a point of going ahead of the cortège. The exterminating angel, the Nike of Samothrace, led the black wings of the procession.

They gathered around a grave at the bottom of a slope, at the back of the cemetery, looking out over the sea of headstones. Ciro was deposited at the foot of his grave.

Padre Graça took the shovel and proceeded with the difficult words: "Take from this world the soul of our brother departed. We commit his body to the ground. Earth to earth, ashes to ashes, dust to dust. The spirit belongs to God. This is the end point of a life. In the grave there is no work, or knowledge, or wisdom, and we all arrive here sooner or later."

*   *   *

When? He didn't say. Who cared about boring eternity? Everyone in it would have traded a thousand years of the Lord's peace for five minutes more of earthly torture. Ciro had shown Álvaro, Neto, and Ribeiro that it could be any one of them, at any time and any place. They made calculations, trying to figure the distance between them and the end. It would take Padre Graça some time yet to voice his ire at heaven's indifference.

"Who's next?" he would bellow at Álvaro's funeral, twenty-four years later, to the dismay of Irene, who wouldn't remember that idiot from Ciro's funeral.

Álvaro, Neto, and Ribeiro watched as the coffin was lowered into the grave, Ciro's mortality looming menacingly over them. Who would be next? The simple fact of not wanting the worst for themselves meant wishing the worst for the other two. They avoided looking at one another. They left single-file with the rest of the group and said their goodbyes outside the cemetery. Irene didn't speak to Álvaro and Célia went to get the car from the parking lot. Only the three friends were left.

None of them had visited Ciro in the weeks preceding his death. "I could have sworn he'd pull through," Neto had confessed when he called Álvaro and Ribeiro to give them the news. Although he stopped visiting, Neto had kept in touch with the head nurse and knew Ciro's condition had deteriorated. Álvaro and Ribeiro were silent on the phone. Neto proposed that they make the funeral arrangements. "It's the least we can do," he said. He was martyring himself over his cowardice, for not being able to bear to watch Ciro's decline. His visits to the hospital had given rise to panic attacks, dizziness, and the shakes, and his wife had eventually convinced him to step back. If Neto felt guilty, Álvaro was a well of regret. He fretted about how cold he'd been at their last lunch, and his unfulfilled promise to visit Ciro in the hospital. He was disgusted with himself. Ribeiro was the last to give up. He had visited his friend until they sedated him. On two occasions, he had stayed in the room for over an hour, listening to Ciro's steady breathing and the beeps from the equipment. There was no use insisting; he preferred to reflect on his friend's tragedy out of doors, looking at the sea and the soaring gulls.

They hugged one another, ashamed. They had betrayed their friend. And now they were trying to redeem themselves, taking care of what was left of him. They would see each other a week later, at the seventh day mass, but there was no longer any sign of their old intimacy.

It had ended there.

Neto, unable to bear his wife's absence, would sink into depression the following year. Álvaro and Ribeiro would still try and catch a movie together, with pathetic results. At Neto's funeral, they would exchange formal waves. A veiled competition, which had begun at Ciro's wake and had been exacerbated by Neto's death, had placed them on opposing sides. The mere existence of one threatened the survival of the other. Álvaro was sure he'd be first; Ribeiro had no doubt about it. His physical superiority placed him at an advantage and he revealed an arrogance that was entirely new to him. They were both wrong in their predictions. Decades later, when they crossed paths on Rua Francisco Sá, having forgotten their rivalry, they talked about getting together, but Ribeiro died of a heart attack the next day.

They bade each other farewell with embarrassed hugs and left, heads hanging. Neto hailed a cab, but decided not to take it. Álvaro and Ribeiro stopped to watch the woman in black leave the cemetery. They had forgotten about her, as she had remained at the graveside after everyone had left. The apparition turned right and strode away, bathed in the light broken up by the fence.

*   *   *

The diva continued her long walk down to Rua Venceslau Brás. When she caught a whiff of the ocean, she hesitated, deciding whether to turn right, toward Aterro do Flamengo Park, or left, to Sugarloaf Mountain. She chose Sugarloaf Mountain. She was light, she wanted to fly. She took the cable car up and observed the city from above, the zigzagging of cars, the anthill of pedestrians, the planes taking off for São Paulo from Santos Dumont Airport. Never again would a death take place without her consent. The solar barge hid itself behind Christ the Redeemer, carrying Ciro's soul to the underworld of Apophis. Maria Clara waited for the star to complete its celestial arch. It was her bidding.

CIRO

* February 2, 1940
† August 4, 1990

JÚLIO OFFERED ME a chair and told me to stay calm before saying what he had to. I was silent as he hung the x-rays on the view box.

"See this here? This shadowing between your kidney and your intestine?"

I nodded.

"I can't say if it's malignant or benign, but it doesn't look good. See the irregular margins here? We're going to have to open you up, Ciro. ASAP. I've already spoken to Cézar Fialho, he's very experienced in this kind of surgery. The team's available tomorrow morning."

"Tomorrow?"

"That's right, Ciro, tomorrow. We've got to get it out of you as quickly as possible."

"Then what?" I asked.

"Then chemo and radiation. It's a long road, Ciro, but that's for later. First, surgery."

"Is it risky?"

"Yes. We'll have to take out a large section to be on the safe side."

"How long do I have?"

"Let's not think about that now," he replied.

I left his office and wandered aimlessly for a good hour, my feet barely touching the sidewalk. My last time in Copacabana. Maciste's flexed biceps on the neon outside the gym, Roxy Cinema, Hotel Lido, Copacabana Palace, and the beach promenade. I don't remember how I got home. The morning newspaper was still on the bed, the wet towel, the breakfast scraps, remnants of a life that was no longer mine. I cleaned up the mess and did the dishes as if washing away the vestiges of a former tenant. I packed a small bag for the hospital, went to the window, lit a cigarette, and leaned out to see the sliver of ocean. I should go for a swim, I thought, my last swim. But I wasn't up to it—not anymore. The ocean, never again. When was the last time? At Arpoador, last Thursday, before the persistent pain sent me off on a merry-go-round of doctors and clinical exams. Cold water, blue sky, hot sun, the last sun.

Júlio had explained that I shouldn't be alone, I'd need someone there with me at the hospital. But my son was too young, my dad was dead, my mother was too frail to take the news, and I don't have any brothers or sisters. I thought of Álvaro. He was always depressed, it might do him good to know that I was worse off. I arranged to meet him for coffee. I insisted that it be at lunchtime, as I had something to tell him. Already regretting it, I placed the phone on the hook. Álvaro was singularly selfish, mean, and cowardly. He'd never do anything for me, much less sleep on a tiny sofa beside someone who was terminally ill. I needed Ruth.

—

I don't know why I did what I did. It was instinct, my dick, my head, the head of my dick. I don't know. But the moment Júlio handed down my sentence, I realized that I'd begun to die way back at Irene's cousin's party, when I locked eyes with Ruth and we were sucked into the maelstrom.

I dialed the old number, the sequence I knew by heart. I hadn't dared dial it for four years. Raquel answered. I hung up. I went to meet Álvaro. The restaurant was empty, lunch service almost over. I sat at a table by the window and waited. While I was there I said goodbye to the beach and the salt air. The last time I set eyes on the sea. Álvaro arrived shortly afterward. He was strapped for time; it was March, and tax returns were due in. He said he had left a pile of declarations waiting for him at the office and complained about his meager salary.

"So many people depend on me," he argued. "They should pay me better. What if I decide to take revenge one day?"

I feigned amusement. I remembered the form that, with everything else going on, I'd forgotten in a drawer. What if I make it out alive? I thought. I'll get caught in an audit. Better to die in the hospital. I started the conversation there, with taxes, which was the only reality he cared about:

"I won't be able to turn mine in this year."

He looked at me in shock, as if tax returns were something sacred.

"I've been too busy this last month."

"The problem is that you all leave it till the last minute," he interrupted glibly. "You want a hand? Is that why you called me?"

"No, Álvaro. I'm not going to declare my earnings because I don't know if I'll be here tomorrow."

He stared at me, confused.

"They've found a tumor and I'm going under the knife to have the thing removed. I go in today and I don't have anyone to stay with me at the hospital."

I stopped there, unable to ask if he'd come with me. Álvaro's panic was almost obscene. He leaned back from the table as if he was afraid of catching it. Cancer isn't contagious, asshole. He glanced from side to side, wanting to get the hell out of there, barely able to disguise his discomfort.

"Don't you think you should get a second opinion?"

"There isn't time, Álvaro. I've come to say goodbye," I lied. "I haven't told anyone, you're the first."

He didn't look remotely flattered. He preferred not to know.

"And did they say what caused it? Cigarettes, alcohol, is there a family history?" he insisted, sizing up his own risks, concerned with himself, as we all are.

"There's no logic to it, it's Russian roulette. I got the chamber with the bullet in it."

The coffee came and we waited for the waiter to leave.

"Are you going to tell Ruth?"

"No," I replied.

An uncomfortable silence followed by Álvaro's "Gotta go" ended the encounter.

"Of course, I don't want to keep you."

"It's no hassle, Ciro, really. It's just that I didn't know. You should have told me, I'd have canceled everything, I'd have arranged something."

Liar. He was relieved to have an excuse to get away.

"I'll come see you, are you allowed visitors? Which hospital is it?"

That was the last time I saw Álvaro. He never showed up. Right after paying for coffee—he insisted on paying—he put a hand on my shoulder, gave me an awkward hug, and apologized for the question he wanted to ask.

"Can I?"

"I hope so."

"Do you think it was punishment?"

Álvaro came across as an idiot, but he was deep, and tragic. I felt an unconditional love for him. I had no doubt it was punishment. And it comforted me, it gave order to the confusing sequence of chance events that had brought me there.

"If it isn't punishment, Álvaro, God doesn't know what he's doing."

I was sorry he wasn't coming with me. That afternoon, on my way to the hospital, I climbed the sloping streets of Santa Teresa for the last time and saw the wet forest, Rio from up high.

—

It's been three months.

They cut out a third of my liver, three feet of intestine, my pancreas, and my gallbladder, all at one go. Then they stitched me back up and stuck me in this bed here. Júlio feigns optimism and I pretend to trust him. I haven't seen Fialho since just after the operation. I lie, he pops his head in from time to time, on his way to another bloodbath. Fialho is disgustingly vain. He likes to show CT scans of his victim's viscera while describing the torture he inflicts in detail. He should be locked away. He is self-important, a snob, Arian—a deplorable, inhumane being. He disappeared when the oncologists took over. Fialho can't handle the competition, he has an inferiority complex. He knows he's just a glorified plumber. I survived Fialho and now Júlio is free to kill me with radiation.

You go into the hospital with one illness and there you contract numerous others that are far worse—opportunistic, chronic, agonizing. I fell victim to fungi, viruses, bacteria, amoebas, germs—the whole kit and caboodle. Cystitis made me pee blood. They stuck a probe in my dick, a catheter in my chest, and a drainage tube in my lungs. My hair's fallen out and I haven't eaten for a week. I'm very weak. I drag my feet down the corridor—they call it exercise. I need help to go to the bathroom and I'm always clutching my IV pole. The pole, my faithful lover. A clothesline of plastic bags filling me with poison. Antifungals, antibiotics, antivirals, anti, anti, anti, no pros.

I told Júlio that I didn't have anyone who could stay with me and he hired a companion service. I never knew what it was to pay for company, now I do. There are three of them who take turns. Eneida, Gisa, and Maria Clara. Eneida is a good-humored older woman who knows how to be tough on desperate days. Gisa is distant, I don't care for her, and Maria Clara has just started, replacing Lívia, who is pregnant and can't be in a hospital environment anymore. I liked Lívia.

I don't know anything about Maria Clara; we haven't had time to get to know each other. She's young, pretty, and must have a boyfriend. I've been spaced out. The fungus is in my lungs, the cystitis has reached my kidneys, and I still have dozens of sessions of chemo to go. They upped my morphine dosage this week. Júlio didn't tell me anything, and he didn't need to, because I know when I'm high. And hurting. Which is why I'm down, because I'm hurting. Sílvio would like that. I anxiously await my next dose and exaggerate what I'm feeling, to see if they'll double it. Nothing more terrifying than a whole day of being bedridden ahead of you, followed by a night of poor sleep. God bless morphine, relief for the pain and the idling hours.

Why does it take so long? I want to switch off, forget, get out of here.

*   *   *

I woke up beside Ruth; it was a day like every other. But I woke up before her, which wasn't normal. I just lay there, looking at her. There wasn't a square inch of that woman that I didn't know. I had visited every crease and orifice of her. For so many years we had explored new territories in an infinite succession of first times. The elevator was just the beginning of it all. When we became mature lovers, married and uninhibited, the desire to start a family gave us a second wind. We fucked solemnly, with emotion. And her breasts full of milk, and the joy of having made someone who was half-her, half-me, it all washed over us like a warm wave for so many years. But that day, staring at her in bed, I realized there was nothing left to be discovered. She still looked good, it had nothing to do with appearance. I was surprised to discover that nothing in me, not a single hair or pore, not one, miserable cell, longed for her in the slightest. Ruth opened her eyes and was surprised to see me awake. She smiled. I got up to start the day.

"Is something wrong?"

"Nope."

"I know you."

That was the problem with Ruth—we knew each other too well.

After work I called Neto and we met at Amarelinho. Sílvio had just separated and Álvaro was still with Irene, who was Ruth's confidant, and I didn't want anything to get back to Ruth.

"Do you still like having sex with Célia?" I asked.

Neto was surprised at the bluntness of the question, laughed, thought about it, then replied sincerely.

"I don't think about it, I guess so, I don't know. This is my life, I don't have any other."

"But don't you miss the unknown, Neto? The chase? The danger? The anonymous sex? Uncertainty about the next time?"

He explained that he felt a familiar affection for Célia, he liked the tidy house, seeing his kids leave for school, and having someone to sleep beside.

"The sex is good. The sex is still good. It's a little methodical, it's true, mechanical, but it always has been. Célia's very conventional. It's the same ritual, which works for both of us: we come together, I know how to wait for her, I think I'm satisfied. I must be, because I don't think about it."

The sickness was mine. I suspected that the romantic fury that devoured me in the elevator had come to collect now, so many years later. I wouldn't be able to survive with Neto's resignation.

I opened the door of the apartment. I wasn't myself, I was someone else. She noticed and asked if everything was okay. I told her that I was okay, that I'd already said I was okay, and that what didn't make me okay was the fact that she wanted to know if I was okay. I went into the bathroom, slammed the door, and took a long shower. When I came out, Ruth was in the living room watching TV. João was in bed. I headed for the bedroom, climbed under the sheets, turned out the light, and rolled over, annoyed at myself. Why had I done that?

I didn't dream. I woke up with her beside me, staring at the ceiling.

"I was waiting for you to wake up," she said.

A heavy shroud had descended over us, as unexpected and intense as our previous love, but different, bleak, devastating. I sat up with my back to her, thought about saying something, but didn't. I went to brush my teeth. She waited for me to come back and demanded an explanation.

"It's nothing, Ruth."

"How is it nothing, Ciro? Is it something I did?"

"No, you didn't do anything."

"Then what's the problem?"

"The problem, Ruth, is our marriage."

She paled as if she'd received news of a death. If we stayed there wallowing, it'd be worse—it was worse already. The awkwardness of the previous day had yielded fruit: phrases, fights, and questioning. The blood flow had to be stanched.

"I'm going to work, Ruth, and I think you should do the same. I don't know what's wrong with me. I'm sorry, I've got an appointment downtown, we can talk tonight."

She didn't go to work.

I saw clients, resolved some problems at the district court, dusk came, night fell. I headed into the streets as if there was no one. What if that was my life? Ten years after the hurricane

I was becoming myself again, as I had always been, before being swallowed by her. I wandered down Rua do Ouvidor, Cinelândia Square, and hailed a cab when I was almost at Aterro do Flamengo Park. Princesa Isabel, I said. I got out at Frank's Bar. I sat on a sofa at the back. Two naked girls were gyrating and bending over on the stage. I ordered a whiskey and just let myself be. I was free. One girl asked if she could sit with me, but I wanted to be by myself, so she turned and went to a table by the stage, where a guy with a beard was drinking Campari. The strippers finished their number and a couple came on holding a faded sheet. They were married—it was obvious they were married, you could see it in the passive way they spread out the sheet and lay down on the stage. It was a sad scene. He wasn't all that into it, which meant he had to squeeze the base of his dick to keep it erect. She wasn't pretty and had a small, banal body, like so many others. It must have been the umpteenth time they'd fucked that day. And although they were being paid to have sex, their faces were expressionless, bored, cold. Intimacy destroys the libido, I was certain. That was Ruth and I. The two of us. What marriage had done to us. There's no going back, I thought. I left a tip on the table, stood, and exited the club feeling restless. Thank God for car exhaust. I hurried to a public phone and called Sílvio. We arranged to meet at Antonio's Bar. I got there first. The same old rowdy mob. Free men, as I wanted to be again. One, red from too much malt, was euphorically narrating how Tarso de Castro had hit on Candice Bergen. Where have I been all these years? I thought. Everyone screwing everyone else, and here I am in this dead-end fidelity.

Sílvio arrived in high spirits. He was meeting someone later. He was radiant, as I hadn't seen him in a long time.

"'Sup, Ciro?"

"You tell me . . . How's single life treating you?"

"If it gets any better, it'll spoil it."

And he chortled as he waved the head waiter over.

"A Black Label, please. So how's that storybook romance of yours? Make me jealous."

"It's fine," I said. I didn't want to talk about Ruth.

"Your life's so perfect, Ciro, that sometimes I want to spit in your face."

Sílvio gave a brotherly laugh, shaking the ice in his glass, then took a sip and changed tone. He leaned over the table and signaled for me to do the same.

"If I tell you something, promise you won't tell anyone?"

I promised. Sílvio gave a naughty smile.

"I'm counting on you, man, you promised! It's a big deal. Old Sílvio here is enjoying springtime, Ciro. I survived the harsh winter. After putting up with the mother-in-law's mug, Norma's prayers, those annoying kids, the smell of garlic at breakfast, I'm myself again, Ciro. If I'd stayed in that marriage, Ciro, I'd have become a eunuch; my dick would've shrunk, withered into a raisin. Neto can take it 'cause he's got more than he needs, but I can't afford to waste any. You're lucky, you married Ruth, but I got sick of Norma in a month. I stuck around because she was still in working condition, but we've got zip in common. And, now, here's the secret. You listening?"

"I'm listening."

"The shit hit the fan because a snob from Ribeirão squealed to Norma's mother that I was having an affair with a hippie from Bauru. Know who the hippie from Bauru is, Ciro?"

"No, Sílvio, I don't know who the hippie from Bauru is."

"Secret?"

"Secret."

"Don't you want to guess?"

"No."

"It's Suzana."

"Suzana who?"

"What do you mean, 'Suzana who?'"

"The Suzana with the joint. Ribeiro's Suzana, for fuck's sake!"

The revelation came as no surprise. From Sílvio, you could expect anything, and from that girl, nothing less. But the bit about the eunuch really got to me. A vision of castration.

"It's her that I'm going to meet. Her and a friend of hers, Brites."

And he made a repugnant, snakelike movement with his tongue to indicate that he was sleeping with both of them. I'd always found Sílvio's way of talking about sex disgusting. Whenever he drank, he'd get all handsy with everyone, very suspicious. My idea of happiness was different to his. Certainly more conservative. I never humiliated my friends for being what I was. I was born ridiculously good-looking, and a nice guy—women shook with anticipation, without any effort on my part. I'd been locked in a stable for ten years, but not anymore. Sílvio was right.

"To springtime!" we toasted.

We left Antonio's Bar tipsy and went on foot to the restaurant where Suzana was having seafood with Brites.

"Mussels . . . " he said slyly, opening an imaginary shell and repeating the reptile tongue.

"I get it, Sílvio."

"From there, they're going to a party that some theater folk are throwing. You're not going home tonight, Ciro, I forbid you. Tomorrow, have Ruth call me and I'll tell her why a stud like you has to be shared with the rest of humanity."

"Tell her, Sílvio, you tell her that."

We met Suzana and Brites at the restaurant and went to an old mansion in Santa Teresa.

The world had changed a lot since the last time I'd been out. The androgyny was alarming. Creatures both male and female. Everyone feeling up anyone within reach. I turned down the quaalude that Sílvio offered me; I thought it best to stay sober. As soon as we got there, two queers who made their living sewing fanny packs came over with languid eyes, asking if there was more where I came from. I laughed and they gave little squeals. A flock of stocky girlfriends heard the call and crowded around to admire me with endlessly wandering hands. Sílvio came to my rescue and shooed them away, saying I needed to breathe. We headed to the dance floor, where they were playing Rita Lee. I couldn't keep up. I watched from a corner. I thought about Ruth, at home, crazy without me. Standing near the railing of the run-down mansion in Santa Teresa, I thought about going home, begging Ruth's forgiveness, and forgetting that fateful morning on which I'd woken up before her. Sílvio reappeared with vodka.

"Having fun, Ciro?"

"Trying. I left Ruth, Sílvio, I left her at home and slammed the door behind me. I can't go home."

His eyes bulged.

"Left her for real? Or just kind of?"

"No, I don't think so, not yet. I don't know."

"My friend, 'I don't know' is the most exhausting phase of any separation, the rest comes naturally. I'm confused, I thought you and Ruth were immune to temptation. Think about it, Ciro, there'll be women throwing themselves at you," he exclaimed prophetically, "but can you handle seeing Ruth single? Think about it. Are you going to hand it all to someone else on a platter? Watch out for Ribeiro!"

"What about Ribeiro?"

"It's just a hunch, but I'm pretty sure Ribeiro's always had the hots for your wife," he said as he dragged me towards the door. "But let's not waste this crisis of yours!"

Suzana and Brites appeared out of nowhere and we went into the stuffy interior. The air of the dimly lit house smelled of marijuana. Some people were groping one another on the sofa, passing a joint from mouth to mouth. My head was spinning from Sílvio's revelation. Ribeiro wanted to fuck Ruth. Ribeiro was going to fuck Ruth, Ribeiro could have been fucking Ruth at that very moment, while I was wandering around a hippie party. We went around the line for the bathroom and climbed a flight of stairs packed with men and women covered in glitter. On the second floor was a short corridor with several doors at the end.

"Pick one," said Sílvio.

"What?"

"Whaddya mean, 'what'? Pick a door, for fuck's sake. Today's the day, Ciro!"

Suzana and Brites laughed knowingly. I chose the one in the middle, for the sake of it, focused on my jealousy of Ruth. Suzana and Brites turned the door handle and Sílvio, before going in, gave me a naughty little wave.

"See you soon," he said.

We went in. Pitch black, moans, and the shock of the air-conditioning. Someone grabbed my balls, a tongue darted into my ear, and an insistent hand tried to pull my pants down. I repelled, as best I could, a mustache that was trying to violate my mouth. I was disgusted by the funky smell of the room, the tantric incense, the absence of male and female, of Ruth. I fought my way out of the hungry tentacles and twisted the hand that insisted on feeling me up. Then I bolted down the hill to the streetcar line and went home in a cab that was falling to pieces. It felt like we'd never get there. I raced upstairs, almost bowled the door down, and sped down the corridor calling her name. The bedroom. Ruth standing there.

"My name's Ciro," I said. "I'm a lawyer, I'm married, I have a son, and no one is going to take you away from me."

And I pulled her to me like I did the first time. It's over, I thought. It's over. Forgive me, Ruth. It won't happen again.

She was stupid and short. Mediocre, servile, and loose. She wasn't worth a hair on Ruth's head. The office Christmas bash was a riot; I got smashed, I don't remember much. Cinira came at me hungrily and I was amused by that clumsy little pig undoing my belt and calling me sir. It had nothing to do with love, it was just a bit of fun. I laughed as she battled her way out of her tight clothing. She got stuck in her Lastex top and I got her out with a series of jolts. We exchanged a few wet kisses with her head still stuck in the sleeve and finally had a breather when we pulled the last tuft of hair out of the collar button. When I looked at her, short, naked, and anxious with excitement, I grabbed that barrel body and finished in half a second. Shitty drunk sex, which cost me an entire night of laments and accusations. I said that Cinira was no one, it was the booze, a slip-up, it had nothing to do with us, it wouldn't happen again, but it made no difference.

Ruth seemed about to lose it again, and I couldn't take it. She should have had more dignity, showed some self-respect, had some revenge sex, gone to Ribeiro. But no, she preferred to play the victim, a pain in the ass.

"Ruth," I said, "you're a pain in the asssssss!"

And I rolled over, I needed to sleep. I ended up catching about two hours of shut-eye on the sofa in the study and woke up with a stiff neck. I was still annoyed at her. I hoisted myself up, got a change of clothes, and left without saying where I was going. I didn't show up for Christmas or New Year's Eve.

Ruth was admitted to the clinic on the morning of January 1.

Sílvio took me in. I spent New Year's Eve of 1980 with him, Suzana and Brites. They introduced me to Marta and, at midnight, we jumped seven waves at Leme Beach. She was dead set on having sex with me in the water. It was a superstition of hers, and I did as she wished. At least I've made one woman happy, I thought. Then we all went back to Glória. I woke up with a hangover, feeling guilty about what I'd done. Later in the afternoon I stopped by the apartment, where the maid told me that João was with his grandparents and Ruth had gone to the hospital with her sister.

Raquel kicked me out. Ruth was sedated. I waited in reception, lost, then went back upstairs and convinced my sister-in-law to leave. Ruth didn't wake up until the next morning, thirsty. When she saw me, she burst into tears. I embraced her, lay down beside her, and swore I'd never do it again. She fell asleep with her head on my shoulder. When we went home, I made a point of carrying her into the bedroom in my arms. We loved one another like newlyweds. Cinira . . . no way, Cinira . . . Ruth was crazy to compare herself to that nitwit from the office.

In May, the month of brides, I took on a land expropriation case in Ipanema. Real estate speculators had moved through the neighborhood like a swarm of bees. The owner of a large developer had forced a construction site to shut down on Rua Nascimento Silva. City Hall had found one of the documents of the thirty-by-fifty-yard lot to be fraudulent. I sorted out the problem and the truck driver went back to tormenting the district. As a way of saying thanks, I was invited to a dinner. I didn't take Ruth. I told her it was a work thing, and it was. The pretentious apartment, with a view of Lagoa Rodrigo de Freitas, was very small and there was no airflow. Low ceilings, two-by-two-meter bedrooms, aluminum window frames, tinted glass, a windowless guest toilet, and granite counters in the kitchen. The new standard of living that those people were so proud of. Each dovecote built was given the name of a famous European: Vivaldi, Monet, Rimbaud. This one was called Voltaire. Milena came to the door with her husband to greet me. She was gorgeous. I was introduced to the crème de la crème of the real estate world—fat, rich men with Rolexes crammed onto the leather upholstery in the lounge room. I listened to praise, feigned modesty, collected contacts. On the Monday, the secretary told me that Milena, the developer's wife, had an appointment for Tuesday.

"Did she say what it was about?"

"No, she didn't."

I pulled the chair out for her, walked around the desk, and sat down to hear her. Milena was even more beautiful by the light of day.

"I want to leave my husband," she told me. "Do you think it'll be hard?"

I was so taken aback that I returned the question.

"Hard in what sense?"

"Do you think it's risky to ask for a divorce?"

"I guess so. Your husband's very successful, it mustn't be easy to give up a marriage like that."

"He speaks very highly of you."

What was that all about? I tried to maintain my composure.

"Milena . . . May I call you Milena?"

She nodded.

"I have represented your husband; I rarely work in family law, and only when there's real estate caught up in a dispute. It wouldn't be ethical, much less honest, to accept . . . "

"You don't understand. I'm not asking for your professional help."

And she gave me a serious look. It took me a good minute to process. It was a formal, grown-up come-on. Milena was much more forward than me. With God as my witness, we hadn't even exchanged two sentences at that dinner party. We ignored each other entirely, and I spent the evening listening to Rio's real estate moguls' plans to destroy the city. I wasn't looking, but she had come, falling from the sky like a ripe mango. How could I say no? A woman like that asking me to free her from the carnivorous brute she was married to, from the banquets with engineers, the trips to Disneyland. Why didn't Ruth do the same with Ribeiro? Marriage shouldn't kill one's sense of adventure. This was happening to me, just me, and Ruth was free to have what was hers. Fuck "this or that"! I wanted this *and* that. I dialed Sílvio's number at the bank without taking my eyes off her. I asked for the key to the pad in Glória, and he agreed immediately. Sílvio really had your back at times like that. I jotted down the address and time, 12:15 p.m., on the office letterhead.

"I might be able to help," I said, and handed her the paper. Milena put it in her handbag, stood, and left.

Milena and I would meet at lunchtime, then I'd wolf down a sandwich and return to reality. We maintained our routines with our spouses. Milena was a powerhouse, creative, chic. She gave me a designer suit so I could fuck her in character. If it weren't for Ruth, I'd have married her. I lie, I wouldn't have done that. Milena was shot at five times by her husband in Búzios, seven months after our affair. Two bullets went through her right thigh and the others buried themselves in the wall of the colonial-style house he'd built for her on

Ferradura Beach. I didn't know it, but Milena had a string of colorful stories to her name. Right after our affair, she had a torrid romance with her husband's business partner. She hated his wife. We were still together when Milena called the poor man to say that she was head over heels in love with him. He fell—how could he not? Milena arranged to spend the weekend with him at the Maksoud Plaza, but demanded that he bring the cockatoo. The cockatoo? Yes, the cockatoo. It was a whim of hers. He would have to take the pet cockatoo, which he and his wife kept in an enormous cage in the living room, to São Paulo. He laughed at the absurdity of it and tried to negotiate, but she wouldn't have it any other way. That Friday afternoon, he headed to the airport with the bird crammed into a travel carrier for cats, only to be caught by his wife with the rare bird and Milena at the departure gate. Milena had found a way to make sure his wife figured it out, and the cockatoo was proof of his submission. Milena's husband got wind of her betrayal and lost it. There were precedents; Milena had never been easy. But attacking his partner, his brother, was unacceptable. A man wouldn't have it. Blind with jealousy, he shoved a revolver in his pocket, drove to Ferradura, and unloaded the cartridges into Milena.

Our affair ended well before all that, but no less disastrously. Ruth didn't suspect a thing. I was present, a good companion, and I was happy, really happy. One day I forgot that I'd arranged to go with her to a dentist in downtown Rio, as João was getting braces. I wasn't at the office when she went to pick me up. I'd lost track of the time; Milena liked to make me late. My slip set off alarm bells in Ruth's head. She became depressed and took the whole household down the hole with her. Milena became my sun. I was obsessed with her. One day, Ruth, in a fit of madness, decided to stake out my office. I left on my own and took a taxi to Glória, where Milena was waiting for me. Ruth followed me and found a way to get into the building. I don't know if I forgot to lock the door, or if it was Milena—I don't know; I just remember Ruth's face materializing in the middle of the room, screeching at me like a parrot with its hackles up. The insults were so many that I switched off, went numb. I got up from the bed, pulled on my slacks and shirt, grabbed my things, and headed for the elevator. She followed, bellowing in my ear. I took the elevator down to the sound of her roaring. The elevator of times past, her formerly velvety voice, our last time as strangers. How could the world spin around so quickly?

The noise of the street was respite for the senses. The strident voice had stayed behind. I caught a cab, it was perfectly normal, sunny afternoon, Rio de Janeiro, the park, the tunnel, Copacabana, no drama, I actually convinced myself of it. I showered, turned on the TV, and had a snack. Then she arrived, transfigured. I denied it, I denied everything, I denied any knowledge of it, what Ruth was telling me was absurd. I reaffirmed that I'd been home the whole time and, in a mixture of mischievousness, depravity, and lack of character, or something like that, I insinuated that perhaps she was losing her mind. Ruth bought the idea, stopped, sat at the dining table, and asked for a glass of water. Her hands shook as she lifted it to her mouth. Her gaze became blank, empty, her movements slowed, as if she might shatter. Ruth stood, leaning on the furniture, headed for the bedroom, and lay down in her clothes. She lay there all night in silence, pupils fixed on the light. She didn't eat the next day, didn't get up, didn't shower, didn't move. On the third day, I called the doctor and he thought it best to have her hospitalized. I returned alone, João came home from school, we had dinner, he asked when his mother would be back, and I said I didn't know. She was released a month later, but it was different from the first time. She was listless, confused, like a ghost of herself. There was no reconciliation, we didn't celebrate anything. The atmosphere was so bleak, so heavy, that no fun was to be had at home or anywhere else. I said goodbye to Milena. She already had her sights set on Camargo. Besides, she had been horrified by Ruth's tantrum. Milena wasn't sad it was over. She looked down on my married life. Mine and everyone else's.

I endured Ruth's convalescence for months, until the itch came back to bother me. Ruth stopped being a woman, stopped looking after herself, and dropped all decorum in my presence. We barely spoke. I waited for it to pass, unsure what was expected of me. Only later did I understand. Ruth was waiting for me to cheat again, to step out of line—only then would she regain her sanity. There was nothing frail about her—it was a trap.

It didn't take me long to fall. It's easier for women not to think about sex than it is for men, for me. After three months of feeling guilty about the state Ruth was in, I started going out with the boys and was soon surrounded by women. I didn't want any of them and I wanted them all. Always for the first time. Three times with the same one was rare. And that's how I had Bete, Marga, Clara, Ana, Sônia, Cláudia, Andrea Marques, Andrea Souza, Maria João, Claude, Cristine, Gabriela, Amora, Paula, Lu, Paula Saldanha, Ana Cristina and Cristina; Roberta, on the fire escape, Mirela from the pharmacy, Gorete from the beach, Rita and Brenda, from New Jersey; Cora in Recife, Úrsula from Paraná, Brígida from 306; Marina, Ana Luísa and Míriam . . . Biba and Marcela. Marcela. I read Machado de Assis to her: "Marcela loved me for fifteen months and eleven contos." She laughed and didn't understand a thing. And there was no time to explain, because then Adriana came on the scene, and then Celina, and then Simone, Aline, Mônica, and Luciana. I don't know who came before and who came after, all I remember is the miracle of multiplication of breasts.

I rarely spent the night at home. I'd stop by to get my mail, have a bite to eat, and see João. Ruth stopped talking to me. She'd just give me a distant look, like a judge, haughty in her certainty that I was worthless.

That was when I met Lílian. Lílian was a professor of literature at the Pontifical Catholic University. It was the most serious affair I had. I missed having a decent conversation with a decent woman. Something besides fornication and the vote of silence that Ruth had imposed on me. Lílian was cultured, unlike the others, and a dedicated lover. I started sleeping at her place regularly. I'd go home to drop off my laundry and leave quickly, increasingly hurt by Ruth. I was responsible for the horror we were going through, but she had taken the reins and pointed the cart at the gorge. She ruled out any possibility of love, cut me out of her life, and closed up like an oyster. Ruth was frighteningly passive. She didn't want to be mine anymore, nor would she let go of me. She wanted me to leave her. The ultimate proof of my inability to love.

If that's the way it's going to be, I thought, then so be it. I found a place to live, a place where I could be with Lílian, with my records, my books. A small penthouse in Santa Clara became available. A work colleague had gotten married and wanted out of the rental contract. I took it. I didn't tell Ruth. Bit by bit, I started taking the few things I had the right to: a few childhood belongings, my books from university, my Grappelli, João Gilberto, Beatles, and Cat Stevens LPs.

Lílian helped me arrange everything, and chose the new oven—she liked cooking. One day, I realized we were heading for a stable relationship. It was a sunny Sunday, after the beach. We showered, had sex, I put the TV on to watch the game, and sat down for lunch. Lílian appeared from the kitchen with a roasted chicken fresh out of the oven, placed it on the neatly arranged table, served me, served herself, and began to chew. I froze. I didn't touch the food, I didn't dare; I could never betray Ruth like that. Lílian moved on to dessert without noticing my irritation. When she got up to make coffee, I held her arm and said it wasn't necessary. She looked at me in surprise.

"I don't want to start all over again, Lílian. I just left my family and here I am already, with you making coffee for me. You won't like getting to know me. I killed my wife. Maybe you're tougher than her, but if that's the case, you're not the one for me. I love Ruth's sick love for me, and I'd love you if you felt the same. But something tells me that if you were in Ruth's shoes, you'd have sent me on my way. So I'm sending you on your way. I'm not falling into the trap of roasted chicken, the illusion of having a better half, a soul mate, all that nonsense people make up to bring us to ruin. The sex will get worse, then the bad moods will start, the boredom, the aggression, the fights. Better to stop here."

Lílian picked up her handbag and gazed at me in shock. She was still too young to see how dark it was in the well, but she took my warning seriously and kept her distance. I never saw her again. Alone, in the living room of my apartment in Santa Clara, with Lílian's roasted chicken staring at me from the baking dish, I realized that death was lurking everywhere. The Gordian knot of the original tumor, on the right side of the pancreas, began to unravel, I am sure, at that exact moment, and divided into a thousand rotten cells that spread through my organs and had a field day.

I went on a rampage.

Regarding João, I dealt with Raquel, or the lawyers. I paid child support, always on time. Ruth ceased to exist, which in a way was a relief. I dreamed about her. We'd talk, fuck, fight. It was good, the only way to ease the pain of missing her. On several occasions I wanted to call her to say we'd spent the night together, but I didn't.

I preferred Sílvio's company. I frequented the wildest clubs, snorted more than I should have, and did my best at those insipid sex parties. When Sílvio told me he was leaving for the South, I thought a break would be good. His dream was to see us all together in an orgy, a brotherly bacchanal. He talked about it a lot with me. He claimed it would cure Álvaro of his impotence, Neto of his monogamy, and Ribeiro of his childishness. Sílvio had a serious theory about it. But things didn't work out the way he'd planned. You don't always get what you want. I think he was pissed off that I'd taken the Argentinean into the bedroom; he brought it up on the phone the next day. He was frustrated. Neto and Ribeiro had let the opportunity slip, and Álvaro hadn't been able to get it up, as usual, instead falling asleep in the arms of his Nubian beauty. It was an anticlimax, he complained, before taking off forever. A year later, more or less, I felt a sharp pain on the right side of my abdomen. My skin turned the color of yellow piss, my piss turned black, and they treated me as if it was hepatitis—but it was much worse. Now I'm here.

—

What time is it? It's dark out. I must have fallen asleep. Have they already shot me up? No doubt they have. Where's my next dose? I want to go back to where I was.

There's someone in the room.

The lack of privacy in hospital is abusive. The doors have no locks. Nurses, cleaners, doctors, anyone can come in whenever they please. They talk in loud voices, fiddle with everything. They clean the floor, change catheters, poke, prod, perforate—it's a nightmare. Lethargy stops me from asking who it is. I don't have the strength, I'm pure thought. It's a woman. New. It's not Eneida. No. It's not Eneida. It's not Gisa. Who is it? Who is it? I try to make an audible sound, but my lips don't move. She checks my veins, takes my temperature, injects poison into the drip. My hand slips through the bars of the bed and comes to rest on her hip. It's firm, like Ruth's.

"What day is it?"

"Friday," she says.

"Date?"

"The forth of August," she says.

"What year?"

"Nineteen ninety."

A fine date, I thought.

"Have I been asleep for long?"

"A week," she says.

A week. A week that I didn't see pass. A blessing. If I were in prison, I'd report them all for torture. In prison, I'd do my time and get out alive. Not the case here. Nope, not my case.

I'm at the end of the row, tied to the electric chair, standing in front of a firing squad.

"Give me another dose."

"You're not due for one for another three hours."

Three hours . . . an eternity.

"Hey, come closer," I say, pressing my hand against her backside as best I can, trying to bring her closer.

"Mr. Ciro . . . " she says. "What?"

"Come closer," I insist.

She obeys. I run my fingers up her waist.

"Mr. Ciro . . . " she repeats.

"Climb on top of me," I plead.

She tries to take my hand off her breast, but I latch on and don't let go.

"What are you afraid of? I'm harmless, can't you see? What harm could it do? Don't deny a dying man his last wish."

She glances at the door, afraid someone will come in. I pull her to me. The face in focus comes with a name, Maria Clara.

"Maria Clara. Your friend didn't lie," I say. "You're really beautiful, Maria Clara."

Her chest heaves under my fingers.

"Come on," I repeat, "sit on me. Be a saint, it's my mercy shot."

"Mr. Ciro . . . let me go."

"No, you let me go. Let me go. Let me. Let . . . "

She meets my gaze, thinking about something, doesn't say what, then checks the door once again and, without a word, lowers the side rail, pulls the step stool over to the bed, and sits down beside me. I laugh thankfully. She smells nice. I wait for her to continue, but no, she stops where she is.

"Is that all?" I ask.

She blushes.

"Mr. Ciro . . . please."

"Climb on. I'll call you by another name, it won't be you."

"No, Mr. Ciro, for Heaven's sake."

"Are you married?"

"No."

"But you want to get married. So you pretend I'm him and I'll pretend you're my wife. What harm could it do?"

"It isn't right," she murmurs.

"Nothing in this life is right," I say, and I know what I'm talking about.

After a long pause, she begins a complex choreography of climbing onto my hips without unplugging the umpteen tubes that connect me to the IV pole. The incision on my abdomen is healing, but it isn't a good idea to rest any weight there. She tries to be quick. Straddling me on her knees, she lets herself down carefully, until she relaxes on me. How long it has been since my body has given me joy, I think. I stroke her thighs. I love women.

"See? It was nothing," I say to reassure her.

"Yes, it was nothing," she agrees.

I ask what she has on the tray.

"Your antibiotics."

The antibiotics alone won't get me where I want to go, I think.

"Anything else?"

"Two other prescriptions, which have to be given at intervals," she says.

I have time. I propose that we play doctors and nurses, and laugh. She wants to get down. Annoyed, I say that she can get down in just a minute, but first I want a favor. Maria Clara looks startled, afraid to even imagine what I'm about to suggest. I am direct.

"Inject it all at once," I say, and wait to see what her reaction will be.

Maria Clara draws back, and is about to return to the sofa bed, but I squeeze her wrist and rattle off the horrors of the ICU, the machines to prolong life, my grandfather who died seventeen days before he checked out, his coffin dripping blood, his body riddled with holes from every kind of urgent intervention.

"You have to help me. They're going to stuff me full of tubes, I'm going to die in agony, you know it. I know you all talk about your patients. I'm not getting out of here. You're my angel, Maria Clara. I've chosen you. Let me go like this, between your legs, please do what I'm asking."

She looks at me, terrified. I continue with my plea. As long as she is listening, she won't leave my side.

"If you get off this bed, even if you visit me every day, and sit on me every day, I'll never again feel the pleasure I felt just now, in this gesture of yours. Be a saint, have mercy on me."

A sepulchral silence fills the room. Maria Clara stares at me deeply. How beautiful she is, good God. Without a word, she reaches over to the little table and pulls the metal tray with three injections toward her.

"I don't know if it'll work," she says.

I feel indescribable joy. Concerned that the cocktail might not be lethal enough, I ask if she has anything else in her handbag.

"Just some pain killers."

"Mix it all together," I order. It comes out too harsh and I follow it up with the disastrous argument that, alive, I'd be a problem for her.

"Everyone's expecting me to die. No one's going to think it wasn't natural. But if I'm here tomorrow, they'll test me, open me up, then they'll come for you."

The reminder that it's against the law, and could be investigated, puts a damper on her decision to help me. Maria Clara panics. In a muffled voice, she says she won't do it.

"Get off," I say drily. "It's not supposed to be like this. And you needn't come tomorrow. I'll talk to Eneida and ask her to find someone to take your place."

Disappointed, I roll over and pretend to be asleep.

Maria Clara gets down. A terrifying cold seeps through my bones. She recomposes herself and lifts the side rail back up. She leaves in silence. I am alone, in the tomb. I think of nothing, neither future or past. All I have left is the agonizing wait. I close my eyes.

I think I must have fallen sleep. I am woken by the metallic rattle of the bed. Someone is lowering it. I hear the scrape of the step stool and a face appears over me. It's her. Maria Clara climbs onto me again and I feel the warmth of her blood heating up mine. Like before, she reaches for the medicine tray and says calmly, "It's time for your medicine."

Maria Clara holds the syringe and gets up on her knees to reach the IV pole. Her belly is close to my face. I slip my hand under her skirt and pull aside her panties. I want to smell her. She lets me, as she injects the contents of the syringe into the drip. A wave of warmth runs through my veins and my hair stands on end. Her skin on mine, velvet. Morphine. My dose. The last one.

"I love you, Maria Clara."

I press her against the elevator wall, our voices echoing in the shaft. She's mine, I cry, and drag Ruth out of the circle. On the balcony, we kiss with the same urgency. A bolt of lightning charges down my spine. I run a hand between Maria Clara's legs until I touch the middle of her, then I slip my fingers inside her.

"My name is Ciro. I'm a lawyer, divorced, and it's never happened to me like this."

NEXT

IT WAS ALREADY light out when Maria Clara left the hospital, the sun harsh on her skin. She hated working nights. So many people die after midnight, she said every time she found herself on the night shift.

She walked to the bus stop, feeling weary. She didn't want to think about what she had done—it was done, may he rest in peace. No one had found anything suspicious; he hadn't received any visitors in the two weeks she had worked there. They all knew. A bed would become available. Who would care? It was better for him, she concluded, a migraine piercing her head like a hook. She took out the blister pack of painkillers from her bag—she had saved one for herself. She popped out the black disc, put it in her mouth, and swallowed it dry. It felt good to board the bus and get moving. The morning, as clear as the previous afternoon, acted on her senses along with the pill. She remembered the nervousness with which she had gotten off at the bus stop the night before, hurrying up the stairs to the room. Why did she want to see him so badly? Her attention wandered over the breathtaking scenery, Sugarloaf Mountain waking up to yet another hot day overlooking Guanabara Bay. Euthanasia, death, a prison sentence. Ciro. The image of Ciro, his hands on her waist. Maria Clara fell asleep with her head leaning on the bus window.

She was a nurse, but she could have been a flight attendant. She had wanted to wear a uniform, have men fantasize about her. When people asked, she said it was her dream to work in medicine, or to see the world. It was all a lie. What Maria Clara really liked was to feel attractive. She made the wrong choice. Aviation, perhaps, would have given her a few more years of illusion. The hospital routine turned out to be brutal from the outset: the bedpans, the sponge baths, the fart smell of the rooms. She was ready to throw in the towel when Lívia suggested she take her place as companion to a patient who was terminally ill.

"He isn't old," her friend told her."He's still good-looking, a gentleman; he quotes philosophers to flirt with us, you'll like him. All you have to do is give him his medicine and brush his teeth. The nursing staff will take care of the rest."

Lívia was living out the destiny that Maria Clara had dreamed of for herself. She had married a doctor, from a long line of doctors, and had become pregnant four months later. Forbidden to set foot in the hospital, and happy about it, as she intended to be a full-time wife and mother, she rescued her friend from the horrors of ER.

During the two weeks that she watched over her new patient, Ciro wasn't there. He mumbled some words that she couldn't make out and seemed to hear what she said, but he never opened his eyes. Cold and professional, Maria Clara remained aloof, dispensed with greetings, and ignored the man on the bed for most of the time she was there. She bathed him, brushed his teeth, and combed his hair, always indifferent, impartial, absent. She spent her time doing crossword puzzles, leafing through magazines, taking his blood pressure, watching TV, and dozing. Ten hours after clocking on, she would leave, her day's work done.

She grew to like the night shift. She would leave at seven in the morning and have breakfast with her boyfriend downtown. Unlike the ER, her current job allowed her to get a decent night's sleep, and she would show up for her dates feeling fresh, ready to plan her prosperous future with Nelson.

The nurse's uniform had been Cupid's arrow. They had met at the bakery, as had become custom, he on his way to work at the bank, she leaving the night shift. The white clothes accentuating her curves, the light-colored pumps, the knees on display. Nelson went crazy over the brunette with broad hips, wearing that erotic costume in broad daylight. He asked her out, gave her his phone number, his address, asked her to marry him. Nothing tugged on Maria Clara's heartstrings more than a man in a suit who was attracted to her. She was proper, but accessible. They arranged to go out for dinner. Nelson spent to impress, and she was duly impressed, but later she understood the hand-to-mouth reality of her suitor, who lived on the meager wages of a bank employee and the hope of a promotion. She was bothered by the fact that he didn't have a car. Nelson took the bus, which in her mind stole much of his virility.

Better than nothing.

Maria Clara had left her family in Friburgo to study in the capital. Aunts and uncles, cousins, parents, siblings, grandparents. She supported herself in Rio with great effort, taking the worst shifts, working overtime, whatever it took. Now, regretting her choice of profession, she wanted urgently to find someone to look after her, share the bills, and keep her near the ocean. Nelson wasn't good-looking but he wasn't ugly, didn't smoke, didn't drink, didn't cheat, and he doted on Maria Clara. He wasn't the catch Lívia had found, but nor was she Lívia. Each to her own. She took the only opportunity that appeared and had sex with Nelson as soon as she felt it was safe. She wanted to ensure that he would feel guilty if he ever decided to leave her. She wasn't head over heels in love with her fiancé; it was enough to have one, or almost enough. Nelson was more committed, saving money and making plans to live happily ever after.

Eneida taught her how to address a patient in an induced coma.

"Speak clearly, close to his ear. Don't speak directly into his ear canal, as it can cause deafness. Speak clearly and slowly. They can hear you."

And she demonstrated the technique.

No one had told her about the change in medication. Maria Clara was holding a wet towel to Ciro's face before shaving him, when the dead man's eyes popped open and stared at her in confusion. Seeing him awake, she almost fainted. She had grown accustomed to the idea that Ciro didn't exist. She missed a breath when she saw the mass of flesh transform into a large, indignant man, staring straight at her. Terrified, she resorted to Eneida's stereophonic speech:

"MY NAME IS MARIA CLARA, I'VE REPLACED LÍVIA. SHE CAME TO INTRODUCE ME. SHE WANTED TO SAY GOODBYE TO YOU, BUT YOU WERE ASLEEP. LÍVIA TOLD ME TO GIVE YOU A HU . . . "

"Are you deaf?" asked Ciro harshly, with the little strength he had left. "Why are you shouting? Did someone die? Who's dead? Someone died, I remember the funeral."

He understood he was delirious and asked for water, his mouth dry.

"Won't you give water to a dying man?" he said, already feeling capable of making jokes.

Maria Clara went to get it and returned with the glass, trembling. Ciro drank it and looked her up and down.

"Lívia told me I wouldn't be disappointed. Let me see. What's your name?"

"I told you my name."

"I don't remember."

"Maria Clara."

"Maria Clara. Pretty."

"You think so?"

"I do. Don't you?"

"No."

"Are you married?"

"No."

"Do you intend to get married?"

"Yes, God willing."

"Pray for Him not to be willing. How old are you?"

"Twenty-four."

"Twenty-four. It'll pass. Make the most of it because it flies by."

Tired of the banter, Ciro allowed himself a pause.

"Why do you want to get married?"

"Because it's what there is to do."

"That's not an answer. Why do you want to get married?"

"Because I don't want to go back to Friburgo."

"Now that's a concrete reason. Nevertheless, don't do it. Do you love him?"

"More or less."

"Then there's no problem."

"Why is there no problem?"

"Because marriage with love always ends in tragedy."

Maria Clara looked at him in dismay.

"Can I have something to eat?"

"I think so."

She pressed the nurse call button. Within seconds, the room filled with nurses taking blood pressure, drawing blood, and checking his reflexes. Maria Clara disappeared behind the crowd, sat on the sofa, and mulled over the short dialogue. It wasn't every day that she met someone who was interested in her life. She had always felt bad about being with Nelson out of convenience. She had decided to renounce luck, be a realist, and marry frustration. Now, an entity had appeared from the other side to say that marriage was certain disaster. He had spoken of tragedy. Condemned love. Assured her that the lack of affection might be an advantage. In what? she thought. She felt like telling him what no one else knew: that during a period when she was tight for money, she had accepted the favors of an older gentleman in Tijuca to make the rent, which was in arrears. He supported her for a time. She suspected that what she felt for Nelson was no different than the void she felt when she took her clothes off in the bedroom of the mildew-infested apartment on Rua Conde de Bonfim. What good was there in that? Ciro had only given her one imperative, and it was spot-on: Make the most of it, he had said. Make the most of it because it flies by. Indeed. In the last year, Maria Clara had realized that, although she was still young, she had no more time for sudden or big changes of direction in life. Too late to change careers or find a better man. He's right, it flies by, she thought.

The doctors ordered an EKG, an ultrasound, and an x-ray of the thorax. They took him away for exams. When Gisa came to relieve Maria Clara, Ciro still hadn't returned. She cursed her coworker's punctuality and struck up a conversation for an excuse to hang back. Gisa listened to what had happened, laughed at the fright she'd had, and gossiped about Ciro a little.

"His son came here a few times with an aunt. He's divorced. In the beginning, a few friends used to come, then they all disappeared. They put him to sleep two weeks ago, just before you started. They're going to knock him out again, you'll see."

"You think so?"

"I'm sure."

The news saddened Maria Clara.

"Why don't they let him go in peace?" said Giza, her eyes glassing over.

"What do you mean?"

"Don't you see the torture? They poke holes in him, turn him inside out, take x-rays, wake him up to do tests, and then they turn him off again. It's cruel. Medicine denies a citizen his basic rights. It's unconstitutional."

Maria Clara was shocked. She had been there for over ten days and had never formulated a single relevant thought about the patient. What he did or didn't take was the doctors' responsibility. She had never questioned the decisions of the high command, much less in such legal terms. She looked at her colleague, astonished, feeling stupid and superficial. Gisa was left-leaning, politically aware, did social work, read books that weighed more than a pound, and smoked on the second-floor balcony.

Ciro didn't come back. Maria Clara left, devastated. It would be good to have a chance to be alone once again with an experienced, older man who was interested in her problems. She missed her family. She reluctantly caught the bus, afraid that Ciro might not hold out until her next shift. It was a whole day away.

She met Nelson outside of the bank. He had splurged and bought two tickets to the preview of *Days of Thunder* at São Luiz Cinema on Machado Square. Maria Clara was a Tom Cruise fan. They had dinner at her place: frozen ravioli and instant custard. As always, the conversation led to the subject of their wedding. Maria Clara didn't feign enthusiasm as she usually did. She just noted her boyfriend's cheer. He noted her coldness and assumed she wasn't feeling well. Hospitals don't do anyone any good, he thought, certain that one day he'd free his beloved from the slavery of health work. He would earn enough so that she could stay home, go to the hair salon, lead the easy life of a director's wife, with a cook, a governess, and a nanny at her disposal. They'd have the right to a luxury sedan, and he would let the driver go just to have the pleasure of driving her around himself.

Nelson slept at his fiancée's studio apartment and left for work early. The day dawned cool. Maria Clara stayed in bed until late, spent the day at home, prowling around the phone, fearful of bad news. She left for work an hour early, unable to bear the wait. On her way up the hill to the hospital, the bay provided a dark blue backdrop and the

late-afternoon sun backlit the mountains with an oran-
gey light, the clear sky, the wonders of Rio. The idea of
returning to her hometown in the mountains, having to
say goodbye to all that, was unbearable. She remembered
Ciro and went over the questions she planned to ask him.
It was urgent; she needed to hear him. She depended on it.
The lack of news about him was a good sign. She was sure
he had made it through the night. She quickened her step.
Would he be awake?

Ciro was asleep, and looked gaunter than the previous day.
Maria Clara washed her hands and sat down to wait. She
forgot the crosswords, the magazines, the TV. When the sun
hid itself behind the treetops, melancholy washed over her.
She had been sitting in the same place for over three hours,
attuned to the slightest movement, but nothing happened.
She stood up to put on her sweater. It was cold. Insects were
buzzing outside, so she closed the window, but the silence
was more irritating than the din of the forest, and she opened
it again. When an orderly came to make the bed, Maria
Clara took the opportunity to shower and put on an ironed
uniform. She wasn't in the habit of wearing it with Ciro,
but she wanted to do something special for him. She came
out of the bathroom, checked on her slumbering hunk, and
lay down on the made bed. She stared at the ceiling. What
if he didn't wake up? She wouldn't be able to leave there
without seeing him. She realized she hadn't thought about

her fiancé since earlier that morning. I'm not going to marry him, something in her decided for her. She wanted Ciro to be the first to know.

At nine, a nurse came to deliver the medication chart for the night. Eneida, Gisa, and Maria Clara were allowed to administer the drugs. Dr. Júlio had come to an arrangement with the hospital in which part of the companions' wages came out of the cost of the treatment covered by insurance. The maneuver allowed Ciro to remain surrounded by women until the last hour.

Maria Clara took his blood pressure and temperature, changed the drip, and injected the antibiotics and anti-inflammatory medicine into it. Ciro didn't move. When she was done, she stood there, admiring him. Comas are so unbecoming, she thought. The patient's muscles, relaxed to an extreme, leave the mouth wide open, the chin weighs on the neck, and the skin of the cheeks melts off the bones. God forbid that I should end up like that. Her previous indifference suddenly reappeared. She stared at him coldly and saw herself beside a corpse. Instinctively, she backed off. What an idiot she was. She had nourished the hope that a dead man would have something important to tell her, some light to shed. Stupid. She turned away from Ciro, annoyed, sat down and turned on the TV. A barefoot Bruce Willis was making his way over the debris of a recent explosion. *Die Hard*. Bullets were flying everywhere. Maria Clara let the violence of the film express her frustration at having such a lousy destiny. Why hadn't she applied for a job as a flight attendant with Varig?

I'm going to marry Nelson, she reassured herself. I'm going to get married, have kids, quit this crappy job, and stay in Rio. She didn't wait for the American movie hero to finish his work, and turned off the TV. She set the alarm clock for two in the morning, lay down on the sofa bed, turned off the light, and tried to fall asleep. She didn't think about Ciro anymore, she couldn't have cared less about him. Tomorrow she'd find someone to take her place. Lívia had been wrong, it wasn't the job for her. She'd be a flight attendant, there was still time. She'd leave Nelson, hit the road, have lunch in Paris, dine in London, visit the pyramids, Disneyland, the Northeast of Brazil. She wrestled with insomnia and fell asleep without noticing.

*   *   *

The alarm sounded. Maria Clara emerged from the darkness, irritated. She hadn't dreamed. It took her a while to focus. The medicine, she remembered, time for the medicine. She switched on the lamp, went to the bed, took the body's blood pressure, adjusted the thermometer in the armpit, concentrated on the gauze, the alcohol, the syringe. She threw away the used needle. When she finished injecting the drugs, she felt a hand patting her buttocks. She turned—it was Ciro.

The bulging eyes and fury of the previous day were gone. He looked exhausted, smaller, more fragile. He asked what day it was in a feeble voice.

"August fourth, nineteen ninety," she replied.

"A fine date."

Maria Clara had made such a great effort to free herself of any expectations she had placed on the dying man that now she couldn't think of a single important question. And Ciro, too, had lost his authority; he no longer inspired the same trust. The hand went back to patting her. He had woken up lustful.

"Mr. Ciro . . . "

She didn't know what to call him. She thought the "Mr." followed by the first name Ciro sounded ridiculous. But just "Ciro" was too intimate. "Sir" was too severe. And she couldn't remember his surname. So she used "Mr. Ciro," even though she knew it wasn't right. She felt his hand slide up her side.

"Mr. Ciro . . . " she repeated awkwardly.

She didn't want to brush him off, but she hadn't been expecting that. Maria Clara blushed and tried to push away the hand that was squeezing her breast, but Ciro latched on and didn't let go.

"Lívia didn't lie. You're really beautiful, Maria Clara."

She had never been able to resist praise, but discovering that Ciro hadn't forgotten her name caused her to flush, her knees to buckle, and her lungs to pump air through her nostrils.

"Come, sit on me," he said.

Maria Clara wanted to grant him his wish. She liked to realize men's desires. It was a special request, and it wouldn't happen again. Without a word, she lowered the side rail, pulled over the step stool, and sat on the edge of the bed. What did she have to lose? Tomorrow she'd be far away, she'd never see him again. He'd be dead in two days, at any rate. Why deny him his wish? Needing to feel special to someone, she fantasized that Ciro would die thinking about her. She would be the last one, the definitive one. Never again would she be offered something like that. With a brusque movement, she got up and straddled him, kneeling on the mattress. They loved one another. That was when Ciro proposed murder. Maria Clara backed off, frightened.

"Be a saint," he said. "Have mercy on me."

Be a saint. Forget Tijuca. What a proposal. She'd have done anything for him. But Ciro reminded her that people might be suspicious, there might be an investigation, and this awareness of the crime interrupted her act of kindness. She didn't want that for herself. He didn't argue and told her to get down in a harsh, impersonal voice.

"You needn't come tomorrow; I'll talk to Eneida and she'll find someone to take your place."

Maria Clara did as he asked. She climbed down, humiliated. She dragged the step stool back to the corner with her head down, straightened her uniform, raised the side rail, and took refuge on the sofa bed. Ciro fell asleep. She had gone there not knowing whether she should get married; six hours later she was considering whether or not she should end someone's life. She couldn't believe Ciro's dryness. He asks me to be a saint and then treats me like dirt. Well, I'm not dirt. I might not be highly educated, I don't read the newspaper or those books that Gisa reads, but I know what a crime is. I won't do it. I've done many wrong things, but not this. I wanted him to like me—I know how to please a man, it's one of my biggest attributes—but then he goes and asks me to do something like that . . . And he gets offended when I don't want to. Why didn't he slit his own wrists when he still had the chance? She remained seated, unable to halt her thoughts.

Then she stood and left.

She went to the nursing station. She didn't like what she found there. Three truculent young male nurses and an ugly head nurse. Ciro deserved better. Ciro deserved it to be with her. One of the nurses asked if Maria Clara needed help and she said no, she'd just come to get a breath of air.

"He's still unconscious," she lied, and returned to the room ready to earn her sainthood.

Ciro was in a light sleep. Maria Clara took whatever medicines she could find, mixed them with the morphine, made a cocktail, placed the syringe to one side, and climbed onto the bed once again. She called Ciro, he opened his eyes.

"It's time for your medicine," she said.

Sitting astride him, she witnessed the dance of death. When he came back to the present, Ciro gazed at her and smiled, then he sank back into the unfathomable. He looked happy; Maria Clara was a good angel.

Surprised at her own deed, she climbed down carefully, tidied the room, placed the medicine on the tray, and put together a plan of action. She followed it to a tee. She waited until dawn, pressed the button, and said that when she'd checked on him before going to sleep herself, there had been nothing worrying, but just now, in the morning, she had discovered that he wasn't breathing. No one doubted her. The general acceptance eased her fear of being caught. Confident, she phoned the other companions. Eneida cried, Gisa was relieved, and Lívia, indifferent. Eneida said she wouldn't attend the funeral. "If I go to the funeral of every patient who dies, I'll never leave the cemetery," she said. Gisa didn't see the point in mourning the death of a middle-class man. Maria Clara said she would represent them all. Her coworkers were surprised. The last one to start, who had only seen Ciro with his eyes open once, insisted on paying her respects. To each his own, thought Eneida.

It wasn't long before Maria Clara was allowed to leave. She signed some papers, saw the formalities through, changed clothes, and walked down the ramp to the bus stop. She fell asleep on the way home. When she got home she slept, too, all afternoon. She had a secret. She dreamed of Ciro.

They had sex, she watched him sleep, they talked, they were lovers. She woke up feeling good, different. She had killed someone. She had carried out the heroic act, given him his mercy shot, something holy, divine. She was special. To marry or not, to be this or that, to serve coffee in the skies or dress wounds down below, what difference did it make? Maria Clara was no longer guided by the day-to-day, she dealt in the eternal.

The next day, she put on her best mourning attire, high heels, applied light makeup with great care, and went to say farewell to the most important thing that had ever happened to her.

PADRE GRAÇA bore the guilt of having given up the cassock for quite some time. The only way he found to atone for what he had done was in penitence. He fasted and endured self-inflicted hardships, but remained locked into the codes of the priesthood. He decided to make a pilgrimage. He buried his cassock and liturgical objects in the backyard and set out in a northwesterly direction. At the age of fifty-four, he would become someone else.

He spent more than a year traveling up the map, chewing up asphalt, and wearing out shoes. God morphing into the planet itself, air currents, dense cloud, inclement sun, the moon, and storms. He slept under the open sky, afraid of animals, of people, and was mugged more than once. He worked as a farmhand, felt feverish, cold, hungry, and thirsty. His only objective was to keep going. Life is the journey, Tiresias told Odysseus. Three hundred and eighty-two days after beginning his trek, he found himself wandering around the center of Campo Grande, in the state of Mato Grosso do Sul. He walked into an air-conditioned mall to take refuge from the heat and set eyes on a wooden door with a small sign on it: FOREST. It was an environmental NGO. He went in and was informed that they didn't need anyone there, but that the organization worked with dozens of outlying posts in desperate need of volunteers. Graça studied the list of posts in locations as far-flung as Oiapoque, Boca do Acre, Lábrea, Manicoré, Aripuanã, Parecis, Jaciara. He took an interest in Manicoré, in the South of the state of Amazonas, and read the names of the local ethnicities: Tenharim, Parintintin, Diahoi, Torá, Apurinã. He had received his mission.

For twenty-four years he had cultivated flowery gravestones and leafy mausoleums in his garden of reinforced concrete, and now it was time to watch over the real paradise. The single-engine plane flew for hours over soy plantations and cattle pastures, until it reached the green wall of ancient forest. He grew accustomed to the sultry weather, to the large insects and snakes, to the noises of the night and the rowdy games of the natives. He liked to visit the villages, to see the sun reflected in the clearings between the huts, to be surrounded by the young indigenous women, with their diaphanous laughter and black hair. He married one, and taught her the gospel.

Far from the metaphysics of the other world, Graça devoted himself to urgent problems: crimes against nature, electric saws, tractors, currents, and pesticides. He was fighting a demon called civilization.

He woke before sunrise, washed his face with cold water, dressed. His wife made breakfast. He was going to walk for three hours along a trail through dense forest to the Torá tribe. Illegal loggers had set up camp in the indigenous reserve and Graça had been chosen to mediate the conflict. The finch sang in its cage when he stepped through the front door, and he remembered that he'd forgotten to feed it. He took a small bag of birdseed from a shelf on the veranda and carefully filled the feeder. The newspaper at the bottom of the cage needed changing, so he got some fresh paper, opened the hatch, and replaced it. He gave a friendly whistle, passing a finger through the bars to touch the bird. Graça loved the creature. That was when he heard the dry crack in the forest. The shot. He felt a sharp pain in his ribs, a sting, a burning ember inside. He doubled over, dropped to the floor, and collapsed, staring at the ceiling. A warm sensation spread through his body, from the center toward his extremities. He no longer felt the sting. He felt his belly swell, pressing on his lungs and glottis, his eardrums and cerebellum; the shortness of breath, the blood pulsing in his ears, the tingling, the sleepiness, the tunnel, the switching off. This is my death, he thought.

He stopped to watch.

He saw himself sucked, pulled to the floor by a colossal gravity—he needed to do something. What to think about? A crowd of unmoving faces appeared all of a sudden. The veranda, the ceiling, the cage seen from below, it was all still there, shrouded in haze, while the dead, forming a queue inside him, grew increasingly clear. The women, the men, the children, and the elderly; the mothers, the sons and daughters, the youths, and the sick that he had commended to God. Hades. He was back in the chapel of São João Batista Cemetery, he was the Pope, blessing a coffin. The last one. Álvaro. He wasn't aware of the name, the face was unfamiliar, but he knew that the last wake had been his. "Take from this world the soul of our brother. Earth to earth, ashes to ashes, dust to dust." A refined elderly woman was staring at him from a corner; he would never forget her look of disapproval. Irene was returning his question, centuries after hearing it. Who's next? Graça glanced back at the coffin and discovered himself in it, inert, lying there, finite. He was afraid. He returned to the ceiling, the cage, the wooden house, and the forest. The day was dawning. He thought he heard a shout. A dark-skinned woman appeared in his narrow field of vision, her face contorted, screaming. He couldn't hear her anymore. Where was he? Who was he? A dead man. A thousand deaths in one. He would carry them all with him. Not yet. He buried his cassock in the backyard, remade the march, took the plane, wove his way into the forest, staked out the house, watched. He saw himself on the veranda, feeding the finch. He knew he was next.

ACKNOWLEDGMENTS

I would like to thank Fernando Meirelles, for asking me for a short story; Flávio Moura, for the strong start; Otávio Costa, for coming on board; Arthur Lavigne, for his stories; Miéle, for the inspiration; my mother, for distinguishing between movement and action; Millôr Fernandes, for having existed; Washington Olivetto and Sérgio Mekler for their partnership; Salim Mattar, for the long road; Carmen Mello, for her love and perseverance; my aunts and uncles from Tijuca, Ilha do Governador, and Catumbi, for their everlasting memories; and Andrucha Waddington, for life.

I would also like to thank Conspiração Filmes and, especially, TV Globo for their support in launching this book.

ABOUT THE AUTHOR AND TRANSLATOR

FERNANDA TORRES was born in Rio de Janeiro in 1965. She has enjoyed a successful career in theater, cinema, and on television for thirty-five years and has received many awards, including Best Actress at the 1986 Cannes Film Festival. She is a columnist for the newspaper *Folha de São Paulo* and the magazine *Veja-Rio* and contributes to the magazine *Piauí*. *The End* is her first novel.

ALISON ENTREKIN is an acclaimed translator from the Portuguese. Her work includes short fiction and poetry for anthologies and literary magazines, in addition to children's fiction, biographies, and novels, including *City of God* by Paulo Lins; *The Eternal Son* by Cristovão Tezza, shortlisted for the IMPAC Dublin Literary Award; *Near to the Wild Heart* by Clarice Lispector, shortlisted for the PEN America Translation Prize; and *Budapest* by Chico Buarque, shortlisted for the Independent Foreign Fiction Prize. She is a three-time finalist in the New South Wales Premier's Translation Prize and PEN Medallion.